A MADE IN JERSEY NOVEL

WOUND *Tight*

A MADE IN JERSEY NOVEL

WOUND
Tight

TESSA BAILEY

Entangled Publishing, LLC
2614 South Timberline Road
Suite 105, PMB 159
Fort Collins, CO 80525
rights@entangledpublishing.com

Brazen is an imprint of Entangled Publishing, LLC.

Edited by Heather Howland
Cover design by Heather Howland
Cover photo by Lindee Robinson, featuring Garrett Pentecost

Manufactured in the United States of America

First Edition December 2016

**ENTANGLED
BRAZEN**

For Heather Howland

Chapter One

Would you rather was Renner Bastion's least favorite game.

Scratch that. All games were his least favorite.

He couldn't help playing one, however, as he stared down at his factory floor. Security guard Milo Bautista flirted with one of the older female assembly line workers, twirling her by the hand as if they were on a cruise ship dancing to bongo music. Renner stood in an air-conditioned office, surrounded by silence. So. *Would he rather* be upstairs in his impeccably clean suit, or downstairs, covered by factory grease that seemed to ooze from every corner of his New Jersey manufacturing plant? Considering that Milo and the woman looked joyful while Renner was in a shitty mood, he didn't have an answer.

How you like them apples?

Jesus. Thanks to Milo, he was even starting to *think* in a Boston accent. The man who'd ordained himself Renner's personal one-man security detail without permission was more Boston than Mark Wahlberg at a fucking Red Sox game. Wearing Paul Revere's hat.

And yet here Renner was, kind of wishing the jerk would

come upstairs where he belonged, instead of making the female population of Hook swoon.

"There's a good sign it's time to go home," Renner muttered, his breath creating condensation on the glass. He'd been saying the same thing for weeks now. *It's time to go home.* Not to his two-bedroom in Hook, though. His apartment in Manhattan. Or his flat in China. Or *any* one of the homes he'd rented to keep an eye on his other ventures.

The damage sustained by the factory explosion in Hook had been repaired weeks ago, the construction no longer requiring his daily supervision. God knew his employees were sick to death of his presence, turning their backs whenever he passed through their midst. Yet here he remained, in this town full of nosy people constantly wanting to grill meat and drink beer from cans, watching everyone else live from the other side of the glass.

"What a cliché you've become." Renner reached to his left, pouring whiskey from a glass decanter into a tumbler and lifting it to his lips for a long sip. "Resented boss. Spoiler of fun." The liquor lit a path of fire on its way down. "The one who gets shit done and signs everyone's paychecks. Don't forget that part."

As if Renner had spoken into the intercom instead of to himself, Milo's smooth movements snagged while dipping the enamored worker. His dark-haired head came up, his gaze finding Renner upstairs, that eyebrow tilting as if to say, *want to take a picture, boss man?*

That was their relationship, if you could refer to it as such. Renner gave Milo orders, as he did to all of his employees, and Milo told him to shove it, going about following instructions in his *own* way. His signature loose-limbed, ready to rumble, swaggering way. Sometimes he even winked at Renner while following through, which in itself should have been grounds for firing. Even if winking didn't break any codes of conduct per se, it certainly violated Renner's own unwritten rule book. As did Milo's walking into his office without knocking and throwing sarcasm Renner's way at every available opportunity.

Apparently Milo fell into some kind of gray area that allowed him to disrespect Renner's authority and retain his job. The rugged Bostonian may have been hired several months ago by Vaughn, the head of factory security and an old army buddy of Milo's, but Renner had the ultimate power to hire and fire. Putting up with the subtle jabs and sarcasm had nothing to do with Renner's reluctant fascination with the security guard. Or the way a flame lit under his blood every time the man was close by. Nothing whatsoever. He had a strict set of rules when it came to other men, and Milo violated them all by being his employee. Not to mention being too young...and too straight. Like, chest bumps and beer koozies straight. In other words, Renner was doing his best to ignore how Milo's security shirt had come unbuttoned halfway to his belt and sweat was beginning to catch the bright factory lights—

"Right."

Renner swallowed the remaining inch of whiskey and turned away from the window. He needed to get some sleep. He'd been working on a new contract pitch for three days, and his common sense was beginning to blur. The account he was trying to land didn't want to use their facilities, anyway. Despite Bastion Enterprises' pristine track record, the rejections continued. Why was he trying so hard?

Because that's what Renner did. He worked until he collapsed. Late hours, red-eye flights, exhaustion, coffee, whiskey. Repeat. After being doubted by countless associates on his rise to the top, a fire burned in his gut, daring him to prove himself. It never, *ever* went away.

Yes, work was his cruelest vice, and it kept him moving. Never settling. He *certainly* didn't make habits of outstaying his welcome in one town. A place where he didn't warrant so much as a wave when walking down the street. It was absurd that Milo, an employee who had about as much respect for Renner as a delinquent child for a school principal, should make him feel…welcome. For the love of God, he'd greeted Renner with a middle finger this morning and yet somehow, Renner had been looking forward to it. At least it was an acknowledgment.

Time to go home. Seriously.

Back to the city. Back to sanity. Back to dating men who were available to him.

Why was there so little appeal to the latter?

With an irritated curse, Renner went to his desk and began shoving files into his leather briefcase. If he went out the back door, he wouldn't have to ruin everyone's fun downstairs. His Mercedes was parked a few blocks over, despite Milo's insistence that he "pahk in the freakin' laht," so he would avoid that argument as well.

That was *not* a disappointed tug in his stomach; he'd just skipped dinner.

· · ·

Milo watched the light go out in Renner's office and knew the stubborn prick was going to try to sneak out without him. The guy really thought he was untouchable, didn't he? But in a town full of people who disliked him—especially after firing their beloved mechanic, Duke, and the explosion that followed—Renner didn't get to waltz around in the dark in his five-thousand-dollar suit. Maybe Hook was slightly safer than Milo's old Boston neighborhood, but at age twenty-six, caution still ran in his blood.

He'd been hired to keep the factory safe, and that duty extended to Renner, the factory's owner, whether the dude liked it or not. The army had taught Milo to take his responsibilities seriously, and after a disorganized, all-around backward youth, he'd learned there was satisfaction in being thorough. To be proud of a job.

Responsibility. Yeah. That was so why he was so *protective* over Renner.

Milo snorted to himself and gave a sweeping bow to the woman in front of him. She was sweet, this lady. Kind of reminded him of the librarian who'd kept a forty-ounce in her desk back in middle school. Quick with a joke and loved anyone who noticed she still had a little fire in her. "All right, pretty lady. I have to take off." Milo took her hand, giving her one final spin. "You go easy on the boys at the Third Shift tonight. Just remember who got you warmed up."

She doubled over and laughed along with her friends, who'd stayed behind to watch. "Why don't you come out and give me a spin yourself?"

"Ah, you know how it is." He winked at them as he re-buttoned his shirt. "Hot date."

Milo left them laughing on the factory floor as he jogged toward the back exit. Wondering how far Renner had gotten without him, his smile dimmed. Bet he hadn't even parked that Mercedes in the gated lot, like he was supposed to. Maybe the guy liked being reminded. Good. That's exactly what was going to happen.

Crisp, fall coolness slithered inside Milo's shirt when he slammed out of the factory, the metal door booming shut behind him. He took a right and hit the sidewalk, knowing Renner liked to park near the coffee shop so he could feed his caffeine addiction immediately after stepping out of his shiny black ride in the mornings.

Yeah, he'd been observing his boss somewhat...closely. But not *only* for the reason Renner assumed. Also known as the same justification Milo gave *himself*—that he wanted to excel at his job. It was more than that, though. Maybe his careful following of Renner's movements had begun as a way to keep the factory owner safe, but it had developed into something else entirely. Curiosity. Even…awe on occasion. What would it be like to be so comfortable, so sure of himself, the way Renner was? Being that the guy was private as hell, Milo had a feeling his boss wouldn't like it one bit if he knew Milo was following him…hoping to learn.

The possibility of Renner's being pissed wasn't stopping Milo from going after him, though. Honestly, he wasn't sure if there was anything that *could*. Which was pretty fucking confusing. Considering Milo was carrying a torch for someone else.

That troubling thought was still weighing Milo down when he turned the corner and finally heard footsteps. Heavy, purposeful ones that belonged to Renner. Up ahead, the lights of his boss's Mercedes flashed, signaling that he'd unlocked the car with the key chain remote. Any second, he would be safe inside the vehicle and Milo could go back to his apartment. For now, he would just hang back in the shadows and watch—

Three men converged on Renner from all sides.

Milo was already running, cursing under his breath about stubborn city people and gated parking lots. He was still a full block behind Renner, so he was forced to watch some punches being exchanged…and not surprisingly, some of them were being thrown by Renner. Built like a hockey goaltender, the man was intimidating. He just was. That was half the problem with him walking the dark streets of Hook. There were a lot of good people in this town, but there were also men who wanted very badly to put rich, arrogant Renner in his place, and maybe get a packed wallet in the process.

Yeah, Renner was holding his own, but the odds were against him. He delivered a right cross to one of the hooded attackers' faces, but two of the men grabbed him from behind, allowing the punch recipient to get his revenge. Renner's head snapped back, and that's when Milo reached the group, drawing his Colt in one smooth motion.

"Told you to park in the lot, boss man."

"Now really isn't the time, Bautista."

Milo's smile was tight as he leveled the gun beyond Renner's shoulder. "You're going to want to step away from him. I've got aim for days."

"Aw, look at that," said the man who wasn't holding back Renner. "His boyfriend came to rescue him."

"Oh, come on," Renner said, looking almost relaxed. "He's really not my type."

Milo ignored the weird discomfort in his chest. "Yeah. I won't lose any sleep over that black eye he's going to have, but I would over losing my job." He strode forward and grabbed a hold of Renner's thick biceps, pulling him out of the men's hold. Backing both of them up so he could have a clear angle on all three perpetrators, Milo jerked his head in the direction of the nearby alleyway. "Are you sticking around so I can call the cops, or what? Get the hell out of here."

Milo and Renner were silent as the men took off into the darkness, kicking trash can lids as they went. Only then did Milo let out the breath he'd been holding, his arms lowering in degrees. If even two of the attackers had been carrying weapons, things could have turned out way worse. Thank God they appeared to be nothing more than some misguided kids. In a close-knit place like Hook, sometimes judgment calls had to made about what represented actual danger and what actions could go a long way toward keeping the respect and admiration of people in town. Still, looking the other way bothered Milo. Especially when someone could have been hurt. Renner, specifically.

"Next time you might not be so lucky, you know," Milo

said, turning toward Renner. His usual lecture was poised right on the tip of his tongue, but he couldn't bring himself to utter a single word of it when faced with the swelling of Renner's right eye. "Shit." A lump grew in his throat. "Sorry I didn't come sooner."

Renner scoffed and ducked past a cringing Milo. Why had he apologized like that? The guy was open to sympathy like the military was open to accepting poodles as recruits. As in, *not open* to it. That wasn't how he and Renner worked. Milo had learned to navigate his boss by giving as good as he got.

Letting on that he secretly respected and admired the man was out of the question.

Milo swallowed and tried again, catching Renner just before he could climb into the Mercedes. "You going to say thank you or anything, you ungrateful dick?"

Renner had already opened the driver's side door, but he slammed it closed now, striding back toward Milo with a curious look on his face. "Actually, I have a question." He seesawed his hand between their chests. "What are you doing? Why do you insist on following me? I'm a grown man, Milo. I have the right to get mugged in peace."

"Wow. You just said that out loud." The back of Milo's neck pulled taut at the line of questioning, but he forced a belligerent expression. "I've told you before, this is my job—"

"No." Renner shook his head. "*No.* You're not assigned to me. I didn't ask you to be my watchdog. This is all of your own free will."

Damn. Milo hadn't expected this. At least, he hadn't expected Renner to get in his face like this. So…close. Like the way he got close with other men? What did he think about Milo's face from such a scant distance? "I…uh." Milo stepped back, replacing the gun in its holster on his belt. "Like I said, you're welcome. I'll see you tomorrow."

"I'm going back to the city in the morning." That

statement hung in the air between them like low fog. Or was Milo only imagining it? Just like he was imagining the hard drumming inside his rib cage? "Before I go, Bautista, I want you to tell me what all this is about. We don't even like each other, right? And yet here you are. You're constantly around, worrying about my *safety*. I…" He loosened his tie with rash movements. "Perhaps the differences in my…biology make me seem different from someone like you, but I'm the furthest thing from weak—"

"That's what it is," Milo blurted, shocking himself. What was the point in keeping the truth to himself anymore, though, if Renner was leaving in the morning? "Not the part about you being weak. I don't think that. The opposite, actually. You've got a pretty nice right hook there, boss man."

Renner raised an eyebrow.

"Okay." Christ. His blood was flowing in seventeen directions, his tongue weighing as much as a horse in his mouth. This was real. This was happening. "Okay, I've been watching you. All right?"

A heavy beat passed. "Why?"

See, that's where things got murky. It had started as a way to study Renner's confidence, hoping to build his own. Along the way, though, Milo had gotten…off track. By more than a few degrees. Instead of learning how to be comfortable in his own skin by following the lead of a man who epitomized confidence, Milo had developed something of a crush. Who wouldn't? Renner was concise, demanding and intelligent, and he didn't give a fuck who disapproved of him. A badass who could raise an eyebrow and have employees running for cover.

Not to worry, though. Milo had righted the wayward course. He was charted in the right direction once again. In no world did Milo and Renner make sense. Nor did his boss ever look at him with anything other than vexation. It was a dumb infatuation on Milo's end and nothing would *ever* come out of it. He actually had a *chance* with someone else. Someone he genuinely liked. The man who'd stirred his first attraction to the same sex. Maybe his ill-advised interest in Renner had been taking a front seat lately, but that was a proximity issue. Things would change.

A lot of things. Starting now.

"I just…I have a thing for someone. And I don't know how to approach him about it." The drumming in his ears beat louder. "You're the only guy I know who—"

"I'm sorry." Renner held up a finger. "Did you just say you have a thing for a *him*?"

Chapter Two

Bautista had thing for a *him*?

"Yeah, try to keep up, huh?" Milo paced to the left, then back to the right. "I realize this is something inside a person. Not something he's taught. But I'm not...secure yet. Not as self-assured as you. So I'm learning the way I learned everything else. Watching. Listening. I don't know how I'm supposed to act around him, so I thought...I'd watch you." Silence. Way too much silence. And a lot of processing that would be easier to do if his head wasn't throbbing like a son of a bitch. "But then you had to go and park outside the lot over and over again, so frankly, it's been way more necessary to watch you than I'd originally thought."

"I knew you couldn't refrain from lecturing me," Renner murmured, because really, his irritating persistence had to be pointed out. "Well, that confession was severely unexpected."

Milo snorted. "You're telling *me*."

Renner couldn't recall the last time he'd been surprised by...anything. His stepsister's falling in love with a mechanic the size of a mountain had been more exhausting than anything else. His factory's exploding had meant more paperwork. Bautista, gay? That was one for the record books. Not only did he like men, however. He liked a *specific* man. Which seemed to be the part Renner's attention continued to snag on. Snagging and snagging. And snagging.

Back in the factory tonight—and every day prior—Renner had looked at Milo the way one appreciates fine art. Objectively, because it wasn't for touching. Even if a man went through the trouble of bidding on or negotiating the price of said art piece, it would only be a pain in the ass once he got it home. Hence his no straight guys rule. His infrequent hookups were with professionals like himself who didn't have the time for entanglements. Nor did they have any desire to waste time on a man who still had a foot inside the closet.

Was that the case with Milo?

Dropping the fine art filter, Renner let himself look at Milo. *Really* look. And Christ, there was no way not to enjoy what he saw. The guy looked like a young, undiscovered Adam Rodriguez. Intelligent light brown eyes, dimples, scruff. The latter one normally turned Renner off, but on Milo, it was somehow really, obnoxiously charming. He had a scar bisecting his chin, which caused a disruption in his five-o'clock shadow, giving him a piratical edge. That was what he had going for him above the neck. Below? Renner hadn't let himself go there yet, but they were only a few feet apart, and Milo's head was tipped forward, as if awaiting judgment, so Renner allowed his gaze to dip down over the sturdy ridges of Milo's pecs, and lower to where his buttoned shirt tucked into his belted pants. His stomach was like a fucking drum waiting for someone to beat on it. And that heavy-looking curve behind his fly…

Renner's mouth dried up.

All of these observances could be for nothing, because while Renner wouldn't doubt him—hell, he'd come out like that to the boss he didn't even *like*—he still couldn't wrap his mind around Milo wanting to date a man. Renner hadn't suspected a damn thing, and he'd been reading men and their signals for a very long time.

Maybe he'd missed the signs because Bautista was only interested in someone *else*.

Fuck, his head hurt.

"Listen, you need to get an ice pack on that shiner," Milo said, not looking him in the eye. "The longer you wait, the worse it'll be in the morning." One of his dimples came out to play. "You can tell your city friends the other guy looks worse, if you want. Your secret is safe with me."

With that, Milo turned and walked back toward the factory, moving in that loose, male way of his. Just like that. As if he hadn't run up like a hero, saved Renner from being robbed, then come flying out of the closet. Renner was supposed to just drive back to his apartment now and pretend that this man hadn't been looking to him for help all this time? Had he…assisted him at all? He didn't know. He *wouldn't* know. Unless he investigated a little more.

Against his will, Renner's eyes dropped to Milo's ass, the lean muscles flexing beneath his work pants. Investigating could lead to trouble. But only for his peace of mind, since Milo had a "thing" for someone else. Who?

"Bautista, wait." Renner hitched his thumb toward the car. "Get in. Let's go…talk about this guy. You can ask me direct questions instead of skulking around in the dark like a confused cat burglar." He turned on a heel, away from Milo's hopeful expression, which was making him a fair bit confused himself. "I'm leaving in the morning, so we can pretend that this temporary truce never happened."

Milo's footsteps gained ground behind him. "As long as you put ice on that eye while we're talking—"

"Yes," Renner cut in. "I heard you the first time, Florence

Nightingale."

A minute later, they were cutting down the deserted streets of Hook, its residents either at home or at the Third Shift. Sharing space with Milo was odd. They'd been shit-talking each other for months. Now out of nowhere, there was a shared moment they had to deal with. It was disconcerting for Renner, who didn't have any friends to begin with. Now—as if being seven years Milo's senior wasn't bad enough—he felt like the sage veteran, guiding the eager, young ingenue. Not a flattering look.

They parked outside Renner's building and he let them inside, trying his best to appear aloof, even though a gorgeous man was following him up the stairs. Jesus, it's not like it was the first time he'd gone home with someone attractive. It wasn't even the first time *this fall.* But there was no denying how different it felt with Bautista. The man who'd become his sort of...uninvited protector. Or had he misinterpreted everything up until tonight?

Determined to get all the cards on the table—just for closure's sake—Renner shut his apartment door behind Milo and turned the lock. "Well, here you go. This is what a gay man's apartment looks like. Start taking notes."

In a familiar gesture, Milo flipped Renner off, continuing his journey through the sparse layout of furniture. When he reached the kitchen, he propped his elbows on the counter and leaned, like a man ordering beer at a dive bar. "So there's no way I'll ever trade decorating tips with another guy. Even if I..." He pushed off the counter and straightened, running an agitated hand through his hair. "Even if this thing with Travis works out."

"Travis." *Huh.* Renner had apparently swallowed a wrench by accident. "Right. So he has a name. Where did you meet him?" Milo sauntered from one end of the kitchen to the next, opening the fridge and taking out a bag of frozen peas. "Those vegetables have been there since the previous tenant. Or the one before that. They're not going anywhere near my face."

"So touchy," Milo *tsk*ed, his dimple showing. He threw the peas back into the freezer and removed the ice tray instead, cracking the cubes into a paper towel he laid out. In the process of twisting the end and creating a makeshift ice pack, he stopped, something catching his eye in the open cabinet.

"Blood pressure medication." Milo plucked the orange bottle off the shelf and shook it. "Your name is on them. Don't tell me *these* belonged to the last tenant."

Exasperated over the kick of humiliation in his stomach, Renner crossed to the kitchen and snagged the pill bottle out of Milo's hand. "Yes, they're mine. But we're here to talk about you and not me. So. If you please—"

"My father took that same brand after his heart attack." Milo looked a little seasick. "You're only, what... thirtysomething—"

"Thirty-three." Renner shoved the bottle into his pocket. "Same age as Henry Cavill."

"Who?"

Really? "Never mind." He sighed. "Yes, I had a mild heart attack last winter. I'd appreciate if you could keep it to yourself." It wouldn't be good for business to have a perceived weakness passing from mouth to mouth. God help him if it got back to his sister—she'd probably show up on his doorstep demanding he engage in some kind of art therapy. "I have it under control. I've eliminated the amount of stressful—"

Milo snorted.

"What was that?"

"That was skepticism. You've been working twelve-hour days since the explosion." He ticked off his fingers. "You don't get enough sunlight. You have to put up with animosity from everyone at the factory. Sometimes you don't even eat—"

"How close of attention have you been paying exactly?"

Milo dropped his hand and slipped it into his pocket, rocking back on his heels like the absolute epitome of someone trying to play it cool. Had he completely judged Milo wrong? The guy had been eye-rolling him since he'd been hired by Vaughn. But it appeared some kind of veil had been dropped. Or maybe he just hadn't been looking diligently enough. "Close enough attention to know you're probably better off in Hook than Manhattan. You know…" The hand in Milo's pocket started to jostle. "Stress-wise and all."

"Yeah. Stress-wise." Desperately needing to move on from the subject of himself, Renner leaned back against the kitchen counter. "All right, tell me about this Travis. Make it fast and interesting. Someone recently pointed out I'm not getting enough rest."

Milo's eyes crinkled at the corners, and there they were. Those damn dimples again. "You know Holly Burbank? The singer?"

"The pop star? Yes, I'm aware of her."

"Okay, well, after I got out of the army, I worked as her bodyguard for a while." He scratched behind his right ear. "We kind of dated."

Renner had to bite back a laugh. Or a growl. He wasn't sure which. "Well, you're certainly holding up the interesting part of the bargain."

The security guard executed a small bow, but turned serious in degrees. Like a clock winding down. "I liked her. I've liked a lot of girls, truth be told." He winked at Renner, but there wasn't any heart in it. "But liking Holly and the other girls…it was nothing compared to when I met Travis. He was Holly's personal chef." He held up a hand and rushed to add, "Nothing happened. I wouldn't do that to someone I was seeing. And anyway, Travis…he goes out with men and…I don't even know where to start with another dude."

His head fell back on a laugh. "God, this must all sound so stupid to you."

No, it didn't. It sounded the opposite of stupid, actually. This was a man who'd taken a long road to discovering something important about himself. Now that he'd done so, he wasn't sure how to proceed. It was...admirable, really. He wasn't in denial. There was no shame layered into the story he told. It was the most refreshing thing Renner could remember witnessing in a long damn time.

But admiring Milo and helping him were two different things. If Milo had been hoping to understand himself better by watching Renner, he clearly needed more guidance than Renner was willing to give. He didn't have the time or inclination to become someone's field guide. Hell, being as jaded and disinterested in real love as Renner was, he'd probably do damage to the new potential way Milo could see the world.

"Shit, we need to take care of your eye." Milo closed the distance between them in a long stride, holding the homemade ice pack aloft. When Renner flinched at the sudden intimacy, he hesitated. "Come on, man. It's swelling up."

Yeah. Well, his eye wasn't the only part of him in danger of swelling, and that's why Milo needed to go home. This was a young man with a hang-up on someone else, and Renner was quite inappropriately attracted to him. And the asshole seemed to have no idea. His wide-eyed enthusiasm was only reminding Renner that he'd become a cold, calculating, emotionless drifter, going from place to place and getting attached to no one. This whole situation was an unwanted distraction from where his focus was required. Growing the corporation. Landing the account he'd been chasing for a full year.

Renner pushed the ice pack away. "Listen, your concern is touching, but it's time for you to go, Bautista."

There it was. The eye roll he knew so well. "Nope."

Chapter Three

Yeah, Milo was giving Renner attitude, but on the inside he was kind of wondering how he'd screwed up a conversation that had seemed to be going so well. In fact, he was still kind of reeling under the impact of telling another human being he was attracted to Travis. The longer he'd kept it inside, the more earthshaking the whole confession waiting in his chest had felt. Now that it was out, God, he could float up to the ceiling and bob around for a while.

Until Renner had shut him down.

Fortunately, he was used to the boss man throwing his weight around and rejecting anything resembling basic, non-business-related communication. That didn't mean Renner's asking him to leave didn't…cut him up a little. It did. Probably because he was still feeling a little raw from being so honest. But Renner's abrupt demand for him to leave wasn't going to deter him from the idea he'd gotten when he'd seen Renner's heart pills. Whether the boss realized it or not, he needed Milo's help. So he was going to get it.

And maybe, just maybe, he could convince the man to

help him in return.

God knew he didn't know where to start without it.

Since the day he'd been introduced to Travis, he'd been slowly retreating into himself, trying to figure out how to deal. He loved women. Didn't he? Yes. Did he get excited at the idea of them finding fulfillment with the use of his body? Yes, who wouldn't? Giving someone pleasure was something he reveled in. Did he want to reach his own release with a woman? Not as much as he'd once thought. And lately, not at all. When he jerked off in the mornings, it was Travis he thought about.

Or it used to be. The body he'd been imagining more and more often was just an anomaly. A proximity thing. Kind of like right now, with Renner giving him a *what the fuck* face, he kind of wanted to kiss it right off of him. And then he wanted to ice that shiner.

His attraction to Renner was nothing like his interest in Travis. It was noisy and in his face, as opposed to exciting and nonintimidating. Allowing himself to feel for Travis, letting those first strains of connection grow, hadn't bruised him. Meanwhile, even acknowledging he'd been nursing a secret crush on his boss was like taking roadside enemy fire. Someone was going to get injured.

"You know, refusing to leave someone's residence has a name," Renner droned. "It's called trespassing."

Maybe instead of icing that black eye, Milo could just give him a matching set. "You know, for someone who just had their stubborn butt saved, you're pretty ungrateful."

Renner crossed his arms. "Just put the damn ice on my eye. I know you're not going to leave until you've felt useful."

Milo felt a spark of satisfaction in his chest. It appeared he hadn't been the only one paying attention. During the time Milo had spent overseas, he'd been most fascinated with the medics in his regiment. He'd pestered them into teaching him more than just the basic set of skills they passed on in army training, and he'd always thought if he could go back in time, he would have gone to medical school. He enjoyed taking care of people.

For some reason, that quality was amplified around Renner. By about seven million notches. Probably because the jerk needed taking care of more than anyone.

Which is where Milo's idea came into play.

He eased the ice pack onto Renner's eye and immediately, something inside him settled. "Why do you want me to leave?"

"I don't need a reason."

"Yes, you do." Renner's jaw flexed, but he didn't respond. So Milo tried again. "Did I say something that was offensive or dumb—"

"No." Renner opened his eyes and Milo tried not to dwell on how green they were. "You didn't say anything wrong. Are you always this self-conscious?"

"I'm *never* this self-conscious," Milo said on a rushing laugh. "I just told the most critical person on the planet something I've never told anyone else. Excuse me for feeling like the ground is moving under my feet."

He regretted his choice of words right away when an invisible wall went up around Renner. Great. He might as well try to infiltrate Alcatraz now. But he couldn't take it back, because it was true and they both knew it. If he wanted a shot at turning his idea into a reality, now was the time to voice it. Before Renner demanded he leave again.

"How's the eye?" Milo asked, by way of apology.

"Fine," Renner clipped.

"I have a proposition for you."

"I *know* you do. I can hear hamsters running on wheels in your head."

Milo's lips molded into a smile against his will. "You're always ten steps ahead of everybody. That's why you're the boss."

Fleeting surprise crossed Renner's face. "Stop kissing my ass because you feel bad for calling me critical."

That was the first time Renner had ever made him laugh. In a non-sarcastic way. The sound climbed up his throat and skidded out, making Renner's eyebrows shoot up. He softened, just a touch, and Milo stopped thinking of him as the boss. Less like an enforcer in a suit, more like a man who would eventually climb into bed tonight without his armor. The sheets would warm his skin and rub in places Milo would never see. In the morning, he would wake with an ache between his legs, just like every other warm-blooded man. Who would he be thinking about when he reached into his briefs?

Stop. These were bad thoughts that wouldn't fit into the plan.

Stop calling it the plan, like it's some brilliant war strategy.

Okay, but if it *were* a war, Renner would definitely be the general, scowling at him from where he was leaning on the counter and still—still—he was...incredible looking. Powerful, in charge, doesn't-take-shit-from-anyone incredible looking. Even after a too-long day at the office and a scuffle in the street, his dress shirt was still crisp and white, his suit jacket showing off the definition of his arm muscles. At the very least, he was getting exercise somewhere, because no one bulged and dipped in all the right places without an effort. And it was like Renner knew Milo was suddenly picturing him sweating in gym shorts and no shirt, because he shook his head, dislodging the ice pack.

"I don't have all night, Bautista. Let's hear the proposition so I can turn it down."

Milo smirked, but his muscles were already bracing for rejection. "All right, here we go. My father had a heart attack, too—"

"If you're honestly comparing me to your father, I'll stop you right there."

"That might have been the wrong place to start."

Renner sighed, and for the first time, Milo wondered if Renner wasn't half as confident as he liked to project. Which was unexpected. And went a long way toward his theory that they were just two guys in a kitchen, instead of boss and employee.

"You are…" Milo cleared his throat and tried to sew words out of thin air. "My dad is really proud and a damn hard worker, so if I were to compare you to him, it would be a compliment. But you're young and hot. My father doesn't have that going for him anymore. Also, you like dudes, so… not comparing."

Renner stared. "Apart from you calling me young and hot, this isn't going well."

"You're telling *me*." Milo raked a hand through his hair. "Starting over. You need to relax, right? Your doctor gave you these pills because it doesn't get more serious than a heart attack and I've helped take care—"

"*Easy.*"

"I…helped out with my dad. Got him into yoga—"

"Fuck off."

Milo persisted, even though the general was definitely not interested in his strategy. "I'm probably, definitely the most relaxed person you know, boss man. If you stay in Hook, I can help you out. You won't even need these pills if you learn to take a time-out once in a while."

Renner pinched the bridge of his nose and exhaled. "And in return, I'm going to do what, exactly?" He dropped his hand and scrutinized Milo. "This isn't just a purely selfless gesture on your part, is it?"

No, it wasn't. But if he didn't think it would freak Renner out of his skin, he would have left the offer one-sided. Even if Renner didn't agree to help him in return. Because there had been another side effect of watching Renner too closely for months on end. He'd seen the guy transform the factory into a safe, healthy working environment. Witnessed the man raising salaries and treating his employees fairly, even if he refrained from becoming friendly. And still no one attempted to pull Renner into the fold. To say Milo was bothered by the oversight was putting it mildly.

He also knew enough about Renner to keep the sympathetic observation to himself.

What had they been talking about?

The plan. Right.

"Travis is back in Boston," Milo said instead, confusion trickling in when Renner's gaze cut away. "I left when Vaughn offered me the security job, because it was getting harder… watching him go out with someone new every week. He goes to clubs and wears the right clothes." Milo blew out a breath. "I know women. Know where to take them and…how to touch them."

"You're not going to practice touching men…with me," Renner said, his voice deep. "That's not going to happen. I have rules against things like this."

"Jesus, that's not what I meant." Wow. He was completely blowing this. Not only was he stumbling his way through the whole conversation, now he'd disrespected the man. "I didn't mean *we* would touch. I would never just presume something like that."

"Good."

"You didn't have to say 'good.'" Renner tilted his head like Milo was a science experiment gone wrong, so Milo held up a hand. "Wait, did you say you have rules?"

Renner crossed his arms. "I have rules for everything. Especially dating."

"I have to hear this."

He watched as Renner started to deny him an explanation, but shrugged and changed his mind. "No one under thirty."

"Now it's my turn to say fuck off."

Renner smirked and checked his watch, which earned him an eye roll from Milo. "No one under thirty. No one with even a remote connection to my company. And no one on the fence." He paused. "That might seem a little harsh to you, but it's better for everyone involved if there are no second thoughts or regrets."

Milo kept his features neutral even though all three of Renner's rules seemed directly aimed at him, which rankled more than it should have. "Did someone have second thoughts about you?"

"Did I *say* that?" Renner pushed off the counter in one abrupt movement. "Look, it's getting late—"

"Help me," Milo said, cutting off his boss. "Don't let me look like some wet-behind-the-ears amateur when I go visit Travis."

"When is that?"

Milo gave a low whistle under his breath. "There's no reason to yell. It can't be good for your blood pressure."

Renner flipped him the bird, right on cue.

Milo smiled. "I'll show you how to relax, you help me impress Travis. Simple as that."

Renner scanned the apartment, the grim line of his mouth saying it was more of a holding cell than a home to him. "I'm going back to Manhattan."

"Look, today is Tuesday. Give me until Saturday when I head to Boston and get out of your hair." Milo went toward Renner with a hand extended. "Come on, boss man. Friends helping friends."

His arm was getting tired by the time Renner actually shook his hand, wariness in every intelligent line of his face. Despite his relief, Milo wondered if he was wearing the same expression. Couldn't be. This was good, right? This was progress.

But a voice spoke up in the back of his mind, overruling his victory. The prospect of Renner sending him off to another man…it didn't feel exactly right. Then again, nothing had felt 100 percent right since he'd met Travis and recognized what he'd been suppressing for so long. Maybe this was part of the process. Part of accepting a long-denied part of himself. Having doubts and questions along the way was surely par for the course.

This was the help he'd been needing. Everything was going to be fine.

When Milo left the apartment, though, the hand he'd used to shake Renner's was pressed to his neck, to keep the sensation from flying away.

Chapter Four

Renner woke up early to go for a run.

Doctor's orders, and all that jazz.

Yeah, right.

He'd been kept awake half the night by a restlessness in his gut. The handshake with Milo. He kept thinking about the *handshake*. Every single one of Renner's business deals was rock solid and planned straight down to the contract's paper stock. This deal he'd made…this agreement to help Milo become more comfortable and confident with his own sexuality…it reminded him of that story he'd heard as a child in church. About a man who'd built his house on the sand.

The story being relevant to Renner, not Milo.

There was a shifting beneath his feet as he jogged down the dim staircase of his building. This annoying *interest* Renner had in Milo should have precluded him from making the deal, but the prospect of spending time with him had been too appealing. Even in the moments that passed right after striking the deal, the tide had begun moving in and out, weakening Renner's foundation.

After spending time with Milo, would it be so easy watching him leave for another man?

Or would it feel all too familiar for Renner?

God knew it wouldn't be the first time he'd been left behind for someone else.

Discomfort climbed the walls of his throat as he hit the street. Dawn was just beginning to break over Hook as Renner started to run, not a single soul on the avenue. His lips curved when he thought how Milo would pitch a fit if he knew Renner was running alone in the near-dark. He would give his usual lecture, those hands tucking into his safety belt, pushing it low on his hips. Maybe like last night in the kitchen, he would give Renner that sexy frown and get close, get right in his face with that displeasure.

Close enough to kiss.

Oh no. No. Too far.

Renner realized he was breathing heavily, and it had nothing to do with the run. Looking around, he saw he'd gone farther than intended and headed back.

When he saw a man ahead loading something into the trunk of his car, Renner was fully intending to ignore the person. After all, he was used to the jogging paths of Manhattan's West Side, where no one acknowledged another soul unless forced. The man straightened and turned, however, and Renner slowed to a stop. Milo?

"Boss man?" Milo peered through the morning mist. "I didn't know you were a runner."

Renner swiped the perspiration off his forehead with the hem of his T-shirt. "Is that your way of saying I'm not in good shape?"

Milo seemed distracted by something, but finally answered when Renner dropped the T-shirt hem and raised an eyebrow. "You're... I didn't say that. I like the shape you're in." Eyes closing, he gave an abrupt shake of his head. "I meant, I've never seen you up this way so early."

"Yes…" Renner looked around. "This isn't my usual route."

"Well," Milo said, beginning to look irritated. "You should stick to a route that you know is safe. It hasn't even been twelve hours since— "

"I don't need a lecture, Bautista." *Liar. You love it.* "You're up pretty early yourself."

"Yeah." He scratched behind his ear. "I was going to set something up for later. You know, in the interest of holding up my end of our bargain."

Thanks to Milo's accent, the word "bargain" came out sounding like *bah-gin.* And a slow punch of surprise and… *very cautious* pleasure landed in the center of Renner's stomach. "You were going to set something up for me?"

Milo nodded, tongue jammed into the inside of his cheek. "It was going to seem effortless when I brought you there. Like…boom. Look what just *appeared.*" He sidestepped in a way that suggested he didn't want Renner to see what was in the trunk. "Guess that's not going to happen now."

"No, I guess not," Renner agreed, curiosity grabbing him. Enough to propel him forward. "What is it?"

"A hammock," Milo blurted, turning away from Renner to root through the trunk. "Borrowed it from Duke. I thought it sounded like a good way for you to relax."

Christ. Renner could no more picture himself in a hammock, let alone his brother-in-law's hammock, than he could a sequined prom dress, complete with corsage. "I appreciate the thought, Bautista, but that's not going to happen."

"Yeah," Milo said, turning around again. "It is."

"No, it's not. Where were you going to hang it, anyway?"

"There's…nature." His tone was defensive. "Around here."

Now that was a stretch, but surrounding the local church, there *was* a decent preserve where people supposedly hiked. Renner had never gone to check. And if Bautista thought he'd get Renner out there in a hammock, he had another think coming. Although if Renner didn't let Milo hold up his end of the deal…would that mean the agreement was void? "Listen, can you think of something else?"

"Dancing." Milo shrugged. "That's all I got."

"I dance for no man."

Milo threw up his hands. "All right. You know what? It was a stupid idea. I should have known you wouldn't go for it." He turned and slammed the trunk. "Just…don't forget to take your pills this morning, huh? I'll see you at the factory."

"Wait." Had Renner said that out loud? Yeah. He had. Milo was looking at him expectantly. Could it be that he didn't like seeing the guy doubt himself? Yes, that seemed to be bothering Renner a great deal, if the pressure in his sternum was any hint. Last night, Milo had put himself out there in a huge way and Renner was repaying him by being an asshole. What else was new? "I have a conference call with Hong Kong tonight, so I'll be working late." He was actually doing this, wasn't he? "Could we get this over with now?"

It was dangerous. Dangerous as hell the way his pulse tripled over Milo's slow smile.

The sand under his feet shifted a little more.

• • •

Mission accomplished.

Milo had the boss man in his passenger seat. Correction: the sweaty boss man.

When Milo perspired, you could wring out his T-shirt afterward. Renner looked like he'd been spritzed by a water bottle in all the right places. And Milo definitely shouldn't be noticing that. Or the way his navy-blue sweatpants clung hard. There. Right there.

Eyes on the road. Mind on the task ahead. That focus had served Milo well in the army, which was funny, because he was more nervous about setting up a hammock for Renner than he'd ever been overseas. His cotton-mouth was out of control, and he couldn't think of a single thing to say, when talking was kind of his favorite pastime. It was just…Renner took up so much air, so much space. His expression said he owned it all, too. Owned everything around him.

When they reached the nature preserve, Hook was still quiet, but it was nothing like the small wooded area. As they walked, you could hear every leaf shake, every gasp of wind. Milo could taste the moisture and damp earth in the air, and it calmed him some. As calm as possible with Renner following behind him, large and skeptical.

"What are you planning on doing while I waste precious minutes hanging in a suspended net?" Renner asked.

Stopping between two trees and unfurling the hammock, Milo felt a hot prickle climb his neck. "I hadn't exactly thought that far ahead."

Renner sighed and began pacing in a circle, as if standing still were a foreign concept. "You're not going to mention this to anyone."

"Was that a question or a demand?"

No answer. "Let's talk about Travis."

The name seemed to send a ripple effect through the trees. "Okay," Milo said, then swallowed. "What do you want to know about him?"

"Would he…do this kind of thing?"

Milo answered honestly. "He'd do any kind of thing. You could say he's on the adventurous side." Without turning around, he could sense Renner's disappointment, but didn't understand it. "Why?"

"No reason." Looking desperate for something to focus on, Renner came forward to help Milo tie each end of the hammock between the trees. "This thing is huge."

"That's what she said." Milo made a face. "Ah, man. Can I even make that joke anymore?"

"Yes, you're still allowed," Renner said impatiently. "And I guess if this hammock needed to fit Duke, it's big enough to fit a cargo ship."

"How *are* things between you and Duke?" Milo asked, very aware that the boss could shut him down faster than a door slamming. Renner's famously getting off on the wrong foot with his stepsister's hulking mechanic husband wasn't exactly a neutral topic. The boss man had almost broken up the lovebirds, and that wasn't even his *worst* offense. "Or should I ask, how are things with Duke since you almost made him explode along with the side of the factory?"

Renner sent Milo a look as they pulled the ropes tight and stepped back, surveying the hammock. "Is that what you think? That I almost blew up Duke?"

"That's what everyone thinks." A thought occurred to Milo. "To be fair, though, no one has really asked Duke what happened, either. If Duke doesn't volunteer something, you don't ask. It's kind of an unwritten rule people have for both of you guys, actually."

"Yeah? *You* don't seem to be following it."

Milo winked at Renner and he scowled.

With a muttered curse, Renner climbed into the hammock. Like he'd been doing it his entire life. So easy and smooth. Once he was on his back, he resembled a king waiting for grapes to be popped into his mouth. "I tried to stop Duke from going in. Once I realized the danger, I…went in after him, actually. But he locked me out of the main factory floor. Locked it from the inside, so I had no choice but to leave him. To wait out on the street like everyone else." He tucked his hands beneath his head and sniffed. "I've since had that door's lock mechanism replaced. It no longer locks from the inside."

Milo couldn't believe what he was hearing. All this time, he'd been vilified for nothing? "Why didn't you say something?"

"It wouldn't make a difference." Renner stared straight ahead. "I was still the one who called Duke. The one who asked him to come repair the machine."

"Yeah. And you changed your mind. Everyone fucks up once in a while."

"This conversation is getting exhausting." Renner looked anything but bored, but Milo didn't comment, knowing they'd gotten as far as they could on the topic. "Are you really just going to stand there and watch me attempt relaxation?"

Milo looked down the leaf-strewn path. "This is the one situation where you could tell me to take a hike, and I could actually do it."

"Just…" Renner pushed the word through his teeth. "Climb in here. There's enough room for eight of you."

God, it was embarrassing how fast Milo's dick got hard. There would be no way to avoid touching Renner if he joined him in the hammock. Did Renner realize that? Was that…why he'd asked? Were men always this damn hard to read? If so, he had a lot of frustration ahead. He really should have declined, but…bottom line, he didn't want to. Renner made his stomach ache in that twisting, mysterious way—so different from the lighthearted excitement Travis evoked. He'd watched his boss move around the factory in his expensive suits and thought him untouchable. But he wasn't right at this second. He was so touchable Milo needed an oxygen tank.

"Uh, okay. Cool." Milo eased into the hammock, the groan of the ropes resonating in his belly…and immediately rolled to the middle. Smack up against his boss. And it became pretty damn apparent that Renner hadn't anticipated the tight proximity. The hard line of his mouth was a bare inch from Milo's. Up close, he looked so much more human. There were imperfections on his skin; some of his eyelashes were clumped together. *Real.* Hot, hard, and real. Breathing through his nose, Milo turned onto his back and propped up his left knee, trying to hide his erection, which was almost impossible because he couldn't *remember* having wood like this. "Sorry about that."

"Are you?"

Positive his face was an unnatural color, Milo closed his eyes. "What?"

He could feel Renner perusing him head to toe, maybe even lingering somewhere in the middle. "I told you I wouldn't be your practice dummy for touching other men, but you didn't agree, did you?" Morning air blew across Milo's abdomen and he looked down, astonished to find Renner had dragged up his shirt. "Is that because you need taking care of?"

"That's not why I did this," Milo said in a rush, worried he might come in his pants. Over what? Having his shirt lifted a few inches? *Calm down, man.*

"No?" Renner's middle finger circled his navel, and Milo stifled a moan. "Plans change, though, don't they? Even when the new plan is a bad idea."

Milo's head was an echo chamber. Nothing was sticking and everything was amplified, including his arousal, which was bounding off the charts. All from that single finger rimming his belly button. *Fuck.* "Is it a bad idea?"

"Getting a taste of you? Yes. The worst one I can think of." Milo was trying to decode those cryptic words when Renner's finger left his stomach, the other man lying back, his jaw riddled with tension. "Maybe it's better if you do the exploring."

"On you?" Milo breathed the question, a thrill racing

down his spine. "Touch you?"

Renner's answer was a lazy lifted eyebrow. Permission.

I need to fuck. I need to fuck. True facts. But the need for release was lost in conflicting images. His usual method of intercourse was with a woman or alone. So, yeah, he needed to get off so damn bad, but the objective was one thing; reaching that point was another. As in, he had no experience obtaining it this new way. Not to mention, he was getting *way* ahead of himself. Renner had said touching. *Touching.* And Milo could no more stop his hand from lifting, from resting on Renner's stomach, than he could turn the sky purple on command.

"What do you want to do?" Renner asked, his jaw noticeably tight.

Wind rushed through the trees above them, shaking some dew loose. "Look," Milo managed. "I want to look at you."

"I don't see anyone stopping you."

Garnering his courage, Milo pulled Renner's shirt up, just enough that he could lean down and see...*damn*, so many good things. Renner's stomach, which was nothing like Milo had expected. He'd thought Renner would be smooth, carefully maintained, but the happy trail he found instead was ridiculously masculine, disappearing into the waistband of his sweatpants. He pushed the shirt a couple inches higher and found toned muscles, nice cut ones above Renner's hips, all beneath a layer of solid man flesh. Renner obviously did what he could between long working hours, and shit, it had paid off. But he wasn't trying to be on the cover of a beefcake calendar and somehow, yeah, that got Milo even more turned on.

Pulse chugging in his temples, Milo spread a hand over Renner's belly and traced it up beneath the shirt, amazed when Renner hissed a breath. "I want to taste you. Here."

"*Do* it before I change my mind."

Propelled by hunger, Milo moved fast, sliding down Renner's side. He took a front-row look at Renner's abdomen, memorizing the hollows, the way it dipped and shuddered. And then he dived in, suctioning his mouth just to the right of Renner's happy trail, before tracking down, down with his tongue. Then across and back up. No rhyme or reason, just getting as much of that masculine taste as he could before it got taken away. His heart was slamming into his ribs, and he was starved—*starved*. His shoulder encountered Renner's stiffness and Milo groaned, his mouth growing more frantic at the evidence of being wanted in return.

Oh my God, I'm touching Renner Bastion. Thought it was impossible.

"You're out of control," Renner growled, shoving his fingers into Milo's hair. "I shouldn't love that so much, right? Shouldn't want to push you lower and see if you'll be this eager with a mouthful?"

Do it. He couldn't say the words out loud because that would require stopping. And he was frantic to lick, to gather the moisture that coated Renner's stomach.

Moisture?

Milo lifted his head, and only then did he feel the rain. Not just rain, though. It was a fucking downpour.

No way.

"Shit." Renner was the first to leave the hammock, while Milo stared through the interwoven ropes at the ground, trying to get himself together. Eventually he climbed out on unsteady legs, both of them working quickly to untie the hammock, confused eyes clashing with speculative over the top of their handiwork. Milo gathered the hammock in a tight ball and stowed it beneath an arm, his clothes sodden by the time they jogged for the car. As usual, his boss looked completely in control of himself when their gazes met across the console, both of them soaked to the skin. "I can't say that was relaxing."

"No," Milo agreed, starting the car with an unsteady hand.

Relaxing was the exact opposite of how he felt with his dick swelled up in the leg of his pants. "Not exactly what I had in mind, either."

A muscle flexed in Renner's cheek as he turned to stare out the window. "We should go, or we're going to be late."

Milo couldn't account for the let-down feeling, only knew it was swift enough to give him whiplash. "Right." They drove in silence to Renner's place, which took only a few minutes. Not nearly enough for Milo to feel normal again. Or to stop wishing the rain hadn't started, wondering what might have happened on a clear day. When it came time to part ways, urgency sparked in his chest. It went against every facet of Milo's personality to leave things awkward...especially when he'd seen a different side of his boss that morning. A few different sides, to be specific. But mainly, he couldn't stop thinking about Renner following Duke back into the factory, risking his safety.

What else was there to know about him?

Before Renner could unlock the door to his building, Milo tapped the horn and rolled down the window. "Heart pills."

Relief billowed in when Renner shot him the finger.

Back to normal. Which was no longer anywhere close to normal.

Why did it seem like the beginning of something...better?

Milo stared at the closed door a few beats before driving home.

Chapter Five

This whole setup was absurd.

Renner paced his office in front of the giant glass window overlooking the factory floor. He wasn't even supposed to be there. By now, he should have been back in the city, planning his *next* move. Instead, he was stuck in the last one. The Hook plant was only *one* of his operating factories, and it had been far too long since he'd shown up for impromptu visits at those. Only two nights prior, he'd sworn he was about to finally break free.

Instead he'd agreed to be Milo's older, wiser mentor, which *definitely* wasn't supposed to include letting the younger man lick his skin. Or run his hands in places they shouldn't go. Knowing how incredible Milo looked when he was aroused and unrestrained was only a part of Renner's problem.

No, there was something worse. Renner wasn't qualified to guide Milo anywhere.

A goose egg lodged in his throat, and he turned away from the glass, spying the mountain of paperwork on his desk. The familiar quickening in his chest told him he needed to go sit down and breathe, but he refused. He'd built this company by not resting until every aspect was fruitful and successful. He wouldn't drop the ball now because of one doctor's opinion. Isn't that what the fucking pills were for?

Through the glass, Renner heard a familiar laugh and couldn't help looking back over his shoulder, watching Milo swagger through the pumping machinery, calling greetings to all the employees who clearly loved and respected him. Yeah, Milo didn't realize it yet, but he needed Renner's help like he needed more dimples. He wanted Renner to show him the ropes when it came to living positively with his sexuality, but wasn't Renner failing at the same thing, in a way?

The manufacturing contract he'd been trying to land for a year still eluded him for one reason—and one reason only. The company's CEO was reluctant to do business with a gay man. Those actual excuses might not have been made to Renner, but the writing was on the wall. Even with Bastion Enterprises showing huge profit margins, quarter after quarter, Renner couldn't even get a meeting. No, he'd received an email about Rocky Mountain Ltd. that had summed up their reasoning. Instead of Renner telling them where to stick their multimillion-dollar account—as he should have—Renner had brought in his stepsister, Samantha, and her husband, Duke, to put a more family-friendly face on the company, as Rocky Mountain explained they wanted. But even that had failed…and left Renner feeling like a fraud.

An imposter who had no business helping Milo embrace who he was.

Renner didn't realize he was staring down at Milo, until the other man's two dark eyebrows slashed down, his concern obvious. What was he seeing?

He was about to find out, because Milo headed for the stairs.

"Shit," Renner muttered, going to refill his coffee.

Maybe the burn would help douse the stupid, dangerous kick of anticipation of having more words with the Boston Babysitter. Being close enough that touching was an option. A bad, ill-advised one, but one that tempted every cell in his body. Christ, he'd been keyed up since yesterday morning, wondering if Milo would have reached over and touched his cock if the rain hadn't started. They'd been so desperate in that hammock. Renner couldn't believe it. Milo had set on him like a man who hadn't been given a proper meal in his lifetime.

Maybe he hadn't.

You can't be the one to feed him.

When the door opened, Renner picked up his office phone to make a call—

Bautista punched a finger down on the hang-up button.

"Hey, boss." He hopped up onto the desk. "What number cup of coffee is that?"

"I don't keep track."

"Yes, you do." Milo picked up a pen and pointed it at him. "You keep track of everything."

"Four," Renner responded wearily. "It's number four." Milo looked pretty pleased with himself over that admission, and Renner couldn't help but admit he liked seeing the younger man pleased over just about anything. Even proving him wrong. "Is there something I can help you with, Bautista?"

"That was the plan, right?" Renner noticed Milo's hand was shaking a little as he replaced the pen in its designated place. And the sudden desire to grab it and hold it against his mouth was *definitely* not acceptable. "Friends helping friends."

"Right." Renner turned over the file for Rocky Mountain Ltd. so he could concentrate. "Did you have a starting point in mind?"

Milo looked like he wanted to comment on Renner's

distaste over a specific file, but thankfully refrained. "I was hoping *you* would have something in mind, since you're the vet —"

"*Easy.*"

"The expert."

"Better." Shaking his head over the ridiculousness of it all, Renner leaned back in his chair and gestured to Milo's security uniform. "I've never seen you in street clothes. What are you planning on wearing to see Travis?"

"Jeans." He nodded to punctate his answer, then seemed unsure. "Jeans?"

"There are seven million kinds of jeans. It depends."

"The denim kind."

Renner had a flashback to the first time he'd met Vaughn, the factory's head of security. And then Duke, his lead mechanic. Everyone in this town seemed to have an affinity for holes in their clothing, and the more Renner complained, the bigger the holes seemed to grow. "Just tell me there are no tears in them and we'll be fine."

Milo ducked his head, looking at Renner from underneath hooded eyelids. He dragged his tongue across his bottom lip as if to say *guilty as charged* and fuck, Renner's cock woke up like a hungry lion. Goddamn. Milo had always been too attractive for Renner's peace of mind. But knowing the guy was not only interested in men, but had an affinity for exploring Renner's body, had changed the game.

Big-time.

He's not interested in you. *Remember Travis?*

"There are holes in your jeans," Renner asked, forcing himself not to shift in his leather chair, "aren't there?"

"I guess this means we're going shopping first."

"Right. Shopping. Because every gay man is a fashionista just dying to make things pretty." Renner's tone was dry as he gestured to the abundance of paperwork on his desk. "Does it look like I can afford to take the afternoon off?"

Milo frowned. "It's not the afternoon. It's five o'clock." As if on cue, the loud buzzer went off on the factory floor, signaling the end of the workday. "And we're going bowling with the guys tonight, so hop to."

Oh, no. Not happening. "I don't know which *guys* you're talking about—"

"Duke and Vaughn."

His crack of laughter definitely wasn't appreciated. "I'm not going bowling with anyone. Especially two guys who only tolerate me because they like my sister. Someone has to keep this company—"

"Running. I get it. And this pile of bricks will still be here tomorrow."

"Pile of bricks."

Milo came behind the desk and unhooked the strap of Renner's leather briefcase from the back of the chair. "If you got to know them a little, they would probably like you."

Renner snorted and tried to grab the briefcase away. "Probably."

"Do you always repeat after the person who's railroading you?" Milo winked at him. "And yeah. Probably. I'm still on the fence about liking you myself."

Renner finally succeeded in snatching the bag away from its kidnapper. "Good to know."

"That was a joke." Milo moved closer, closer, until Renner was forced to stop gathering files and shoving them into the briefcase. Absolute stillness was necessary so he could concentrate on not inhaling a heaping lungful of Milo's cologne. It was subtle, probably having worn off throughout the workday, but that only made way for his natural male scent, leaving a mixture of earth and something spiced. "I'm not on the fence about liking you. I'm firmly on one side."

"Which side it that?"

Milo smiled, and Renner's stupid, apparently *masochistic* heart warmed and expanded. "I'll tell you after we go bowling. Think of it as an incentive."

"I don't care if you like me or not."

"Yes, you do."

He reached for his coffee and Milo snagged his wrist, holding it captive. "Enough with the caffeine. Don't make me compare your health to my senior citizen father's again."

His brain took a spur-of-the-moment vacation. Or maybe pride was the explanation for drawing their joined hands to the small of Milo's back. Roughly. Shoving him up against the desk with the use of his chest. A groan got stuck in his throat over the way Milo's thighs flexed, his stomach hollowing to accommodate Renner's belt. "I'm healthy as a fucking horse, and unless you want some good, hard confirmation on that, Bautista, I would refrain from comparing me again to your daddy."

Whoa. He'd said way too much. Milo hadn't breathed in at least twenty seconds, as far as he could tell. Oh, but then, he started breathing *really* fast. Like he'd just breached the surface after a deep-sea dive. "What does that mean?" He shifted a little, his thigh rubbing against Renner's hard dick. *Christ.* "Shit. Okay. I know what *that* means. Are you—"

Renner released Milo—when had he grabbed him?—leaving him to slump a little on the desk, his surprise evident. "It doesn't mean anything, except I don't appreciate your constant reminders that I'm working too hard. Believe me, I'm aware."

"Really? There seemed to be more." Milo's tongue swiped across his bottom lip again, like a taunt. "A lot more."

Oh, for the love of God. Had his cock really just grown heavier with the insinuation that he was packing? Milo's age was already rubbing off on him. *Don't think about rubbing.* Refraining was difficult, though, when Milo was still leaned back on the desk, his eyes just a touch hopeful, like he couldn't help but want Renner to change his mind and climb on. *Fuck.* The guy was starved for his first experience with a man, that was painfully obvious, and not obliging Milo and showing him how good it could be? *Agonizing.*

But he wouldn't. He wouldn't use that desperation to scratch the seriously itchy itch Milo had started in his belly, unreachable save that *one method* of scratching. Not when Milo could be with someone just as thirsty for life as he was. Someone he really liked. Someone who could offer him something beside a packed travel schedule, long hours, and a damaged aorta.

"First lesson, Bautista. Don't read too much into every hard dick you come across going forward. Or you're going to spend a lot of time confused." He draped the strap of his bag across his chest. "I'm going to change my mind about shopping and bowling in three…two…"

"All right, already." Milo slid off the desk and adjusted his own visible erection with a wince, and hell if that didn't tempt Renner to kiss the lingering confusion off his face. *Don't even think about it.* "Let's go buy some jeans without holes, I guess."

Chapter Six

Hot damn.

Milo tried to walk the normal way and leave the extra bounce out of his step, but it was hard. Kind of like his dick, which wouldn't stop plumping up behind his security belt every time he thought of Renner shoving him into the desk. Okay, though. This was *great*. Take away the fact that it had been Renner doing the shoving—which was proving pretty difficult a feat—and he had his first hint at what the future might be like, if he paid attention to the signals his body and mind were giving off.

With women, he'd always let them take the lead. And the women he gravitated toward were usually the type to like it that way. They would push him flat onto his back and ride him until they collapsed, marveling over the fact that he hadn't climaxed…right before they fell asleep from exhaustion. Which is when he normally rolled out of bed and handled his own shit in the bathroom, aided by flashes of images he hadn't always understood.

Until now. His chest was still on fire from where Renner's

concrete-slab pectorals had pinned him. And that thing he'd said about being compared to Milo's daddy…was a little baffling for sure. Not just the actual *words*, but the way his gut had twisted in a really slow, really awesome way. Rome wasn't built in a day, though. He had all the time in the world to figure out why certain words and touches called to corresponding parts of him.

Thank God he had Renner to help him out.

Right.

The guy looked about as thrilled to be walking through a strip mall parking lot in New Jersey as a man on his way to the gallows.

"Try to look a little less like you want to die," Milo suggested, holding the glass door for Renner to pass through. "Just for kicks."

They were walking into a chain department store that had huge CLOSEOUT SALE signs in the window, which probably only accounted for half of Renner's dramatic sigh. "I highly doubt we're going to find anything decent in this place." The store manager they passed sucked her teeth at him, but he just twisted his lips, which probably should have irritated Milo, but he found himself battling a laugh instead. "You know, there's this thing called online shopping. You should check into it."

"You only gave me until the weekend," Milo said automatically. "I want your opinion, so I don't have time for all that."

When he glanced over at Renner, the other man was giving him a strange look, but it didn't last long. "Right, the weekend. Well. Better me than one of your bowling team members." He plucked a black T-shirt off a rack, scanned it with a bored expression and hung it back up. "How is it that my factory sponsors a bowling team and I wasn't aware of it?"

"You might want to take it up with accounting." Milo veered off toward the giant wall of folded blue jeans. "But the cost of shoe rentals might not be the right hill to die on."

"What are you, my business adviser now, as well as my lifestyle guru?"

The corner of Milo's mouth kicked up as Renner came to stand beside him at the Wall o' Jeans, and Milo gave him an elbow in the side. "All these new hats I'm wearing calls for a pay raise, no?"

"Don't remind me that I'm out shopping with an employee," Renner muttered. "This specific activity isn't on the rule list, but it probably falls under the umbrella of rule one."

Milo reached for a pair of light blue jeans with bright orange stitching—just to fuck with Renner—and got his hand slapped for the effort. Again, he had to tone down his smile. "I won't tell anyone if you don't." The little devil in his stomach prodded him into adding, "About any of it. Even if—"

"Don't finish that sentence."

God, the man was smart. *Even if it goes further next time.* That was *actually* what Milo had been about to say. Which was probably the most idiotic idea he'd ever come up with. He'd given a lot of thought to the type of man Renner dated, and Milo was not even on the spectrum. First of all, Renner was rich as sin. Milo knew through Duke that the guy had residences all over the globe. His apartment in Manhattan apparently took up an entire floor of a building in Gramercy. Throw in the way he dressed, how he spoke, his education, his differing interests...and yeah, if Milo didn't work for Renner, the boss man probably wouldn't even look twice at him on the street.

He'd said so himself. Milo wasn't his type.

Milo was trying really hard not to let any of those facts bother him.

Why should they, right? He was going to Boston Saturday to see Travis. Blond, sharp, talented, positive, quick-with-a-joke Travis. Was the personal chef more his speed? He thought so, but he wouldn't know for sure until he got his act together and tried.

Hence, jeans. Focus on the jeans.

Not the man whose voice had dropped so low back in the office, Milo had left his stomach behind on the floor. *I'm healthy as a fucking horse, and unless you want some good, hard confirmation on that, Bautista, I would refrain from comparing me again to your daddy.*

There it was again. That long, slow melt beneath his waistband.

"Try these ones," Renner said, slapping folded denim up against Milo's chest and catching him off guard. "They're not a total crime against humanity."

"That's quite an endorsement." Milo threw them over his shoulder and headed toward the changing rooms. "I'll get started with these while you find me a shirt."

Renner ran a finger beneath the collar of his shirt. "When did I become the employee?"

"It's a nice change of pace, isn't it?"

Milo turned down the dim corridor toward a series of empty dressing rooms before Renner could respond, which only gave him more reason to finally let his smile bloom. Once inside a small room toward the middle of the row, Milo wasted no time shucking his pants, pausing when he caught sight of himself in the mirror. The ridge of his cock tented his boxer briefs, just as hard as it had been since Renner's office. Making matters worse, his alarm hadn't gone off that morning, stealing his usual beat-off time. God, he was hot. That had to account for the ever-increasing awareness of his boss.

Listening out for Renner's approach and hearing nothing, Milo reached into his briefs and gave his cock a rough jerk. How was he going to make it through bowling with this thing? It was going to be mistaken for an extra pin.

Milo forced himself to stop stroking himself and breathed, breathed *deeply* through his nose. He needed to get the jeans on before Renner showed up and started complaining about Milo wasting his time. When he finally got them on, zipping up was painful, but he managed it, tucking his flesh to the side in way he hoped wasn't too noticeable.

A brisk knock on the door left no doubt as to who was on the other side. "How are they?"

"Tight. Uncomfortable. I hate them."

"We have a winner."

Milo tried to drop into a crouch, but the starch-like material prevented him. "You can't be serious." He twisted left and right. "If I'd been wearing these night before last, I'd probably still be running to your rescue."

"You literally *never* stop bringing up annoying subjects." A long-suffering sigh and then the door opened, revealing Renner's reflection in the dressing room mirror. And yeah, he spied the wood Milo was still sporting, just beneath the hem of his un-tucked security shirt. His eyes flared, just a touch, before he went back to being his usual stoic self. Or maybe not quite as stoic, because his jaw looked bunched enough to shatter.

This can't be good for his blood pressure.

Don't say that out loud.

Renner tossed him a shirt. "Try this on with the jeans. Maybe once you see how the whole deal looks together, you won't mind sacrificing your comfort."

"Doubtful." Milo hesitated halfway through unbuttoning his shirt when a realization hit him. This was the first time he'd be somewhat naked in front of a man who was *interested* in men. At least that he'd known about. And there was something exciting and...terrifying about that. What would Renner think of his appearance?

"What's wrong?" Renner raised an eyebrow. "You think

I'm going to act like a teenage girl at a One Direction concert over some nipples?"

"In this scenario, is Zayn still in the band?"

Renner stared, a muscle leaping in his cheek.

Milo slipped a few more buttons free, trying not to be obvious about gritting his molars. Why was his cock getting harder over his own impending half-nakedness? Was he some kind of narcissist now, or was it the fact that Renner was watching? Watching *really* closely, truth be told. Even if he seemed to be pretending otherwise. "You know, the way you're showing me the ropes like this? It qualifies you for the Mr. Miyagi nickname."

"Jesus, Bautista. Do I need to take the shirt off for you?"

Their gazes zeroed in on each other in the mirror. "Do you want to?"

Silence passed by, loping and heavy. "Get it off."

Chapter Seven

What the hell was he doing?

Not waiting outside like a normal, non-creepy-as-shit weirdo. *That's* what. He'd handed Milo the shirt to try on and the activity *did not* require an audience. At least not *before* the garment was on. Shit, standing there broke so many rules, it wasn't even funny. Forming this confusing mentorship/friendship with one of his workers was bad enough, but joining him in the dressing room took the cake.

It was just…damn. That hard-on struggling for breath in Milo's pants couldn't be for him, could it? Renner could almost feel how bad it had pained the security guard to shove his erect dick into the stiff denim. To feign a casual attitude when he was longing for high-quality porn and some tissues.

Renner was the one who needed to be someplace else, though. Not taking deep, measured breaths while waiting for Milo to remove his shirt the entire damn way. How high on his thick arms did those tattoo sleeves run? Did they continue on to his chest? Forget about the fact that once the shirt came off, he would see the full outline of Milo's cock. The fleshy ridge around the head, the exact thickness. Thoughts a smart businessman didn't have about his employees. Hell, thoughts a smart man didn't have, period. Not about someone unavailable to him in so many ways—and when exactly had *that* started to matter?

Intending to go back out into the store and wait by the register, Renner began to close the dressing room door. Which of course is when Milo yanked the shirt free of his waistband and let it drop. And *oh fuck*. Renner couldn't decide what turned him immobile first. The riot of tattoos covering Bautista from neck to waistband. The muscles that were so prominent, Renner could have counted the cords and veins running through each bulge of bicep, abdominal, and hip. Or it could very well have been the wet spot at the very top of where Milo's cock had been stuffed into the jeans. Meaning those drops of moisture had made an appearance some time in the last few minutes. Over what?

Yeah, it could have been any combination of those things that kept Renner poised in the doorway, but none was as prominent as Milo's vigilance. He watched Renner under hooded eyelids in the mirror, running nervous fingers up and down the center of his corrugated stomach. As if he sincerely didn't know that anyone with a pulse would find him stunningly attractive.

"I guess I should try the shirt on," Milo said, his voice scratchy.

"Right," Renner managed. "The shirt."

He couldn't keep his attention off the way Milo's abs dipped and swelled as he pulled the deep red shirt over his head, dropping the material to his waist. By the time he finished the task, he was back to watching Renner in the mirror. Expecting what?

"Well?" Milo turned around, his breath noticeably thinner. "Does this work?"

"Yeah," Renner said hoarsely, reaching outside the dressing room for the casual jacket he'd hung on the neighboring door. "Try this on with it."

A wrinkle formed on Milo's brow. "I don't know about this one, Miyagi. I feel like I'm crossing the line into trying-too-hard territory."

"Good," Renner said with a firm nod. "You're supposed to try hard."

"No holes in the jeans."

"Correct."

"Jackets you have to take to a dry cleaner."

"You'll learn to enjoy having clean clothes waiting on hangers."

Milo looked skeptical as he faced the mirror once more, tugging on the lapel of the jacket like it was made of poisonous spiders. Renner stepped to the side and observed as well, having no idea how to feel about the effortless transformation. On one hand, holy shit, that had been easy. If the guy walked into a Manhattan club in that outfit, he probably wouldn't make two steps before he was in the crosshairs of several interested men. His lack of polish actually worked in his favor. It made him fresh, different. Real.

Too real for the costume Renner had dressed him in.

Watching Milo roll his shoulders inside the jacket, fidgeting with the tight shirt beneath, Renner felt suddenly sick. "Take it off."

"Why?" Milo's head whipped in his direction. "You don't like it now?"

"You look great, but you don't need it. You should dress how you're comfortable. Okay?" Renner reached for the jacket, trying to peel it down Milo's arms, but the younger man slipped out of his reach. "Take it *off*, Bautista."

"No." He ran his hands down the front of the red shirt. "You came all the way down here to help me. Maybe I just need to get used to it."

Renner didn't really have a logical explanation for needing to extricate Milo from the shitty jacket and too-tight jeans, only knew it had to be done. He'd advised him all wrong. See? He'd known he wasn't cut out for this. First task and he'd told this man who needed to change absolutely nothing...that he'd look better some other way. "Look, you don't need to be...improved upon." When Milo's back hit the dressing room wall, Renner realized he'd been prowling forward, giving the other man no choice but to back up. But he couldn't go any farther now. And Renner couldn't seem to budge or give him any personal space. His hands were curled in the front of his jacket, shoving it off Milo's arms before he knew his own intentions. "Now hand over the shirt."

"No." Milo drew the word out, nostrils flaring. Then his eyes slammed shut, a rough curse punching into the air between them. But not before Renner saw the conflict waging itself. The guy was plastered up against the dressing room wall, sweat beginning to shine on his upper lip and— Renner looked down—yeah, he was still hard in those stupid, not-good-enough jeans. For days. Correction: they were *both* still hard. For days. "I, uh..." Milo started. "Maybe we should address the elephant...trunk...in the room."

Renner almost laughed. When was the last time he'd laughed without sarcasm? "Go ahead." Oh yeah, he was playing with fire, but he stepped closer and their bulges brushed together, coiling his gut like a warm snake. "Address it."

Incredible. That one touch had Milo baring his teeth, eyes still locked up tight. His behavior was that of a man getting a blow job, and Renner wouldn't lie, that over-the-top reaction was a powerful thing. It was uncultivated and honest. "Address it. O-kay," Milo said on a breath. "The way you touched me back in the office. Or...*didn't* touch me. Whatever. I wasn't positive I would like a man coming on to me like that. But I did. I really fucking did." He reached between their bodies and adjusted himself with a harsh grunt. "I think I'm just anxious for more. I want to feel that way again."

"With Travis."

A long pause. "Yeah."

Had there been a serious hesitation, or was Renner battling too much lust to be objective? His groin was so heavy, the seams of his briefs were digging into the weighed-down flesh. The ridge of his hard cock continued to nudge against Milo's, drawing little catches of breath that were nothing short of addictive. "Do you want to feel that way again now?" Renner dragged a hand down Milo's package, massaging it through the denim. "Or do you want to wait?"

"Now," Milo groaned, his head rolling side to side on the wall. "Oh fuck. Right now. *Please.*"

Never in his life had Renner gone light-headed over a hookup. Never. But the unabashed begging from Milo flipped a break switch somewhere and caused a flare of wicked electricity. He was unzipping Milo from his jeans using fingers with far less skill than he usually possessed. This was insane. His rules were written in stone. Had they been eroded, or was he turning a blind eye? He didn't know. Only knew Milo's big, stiff dick was in his hands and the guy was acting like the world was *ending*, clawing at the dressing room wall, his thighs vibrating. His first experience with a man.

Don't ruin it. Don't screw it up for him.

Renner used his free hand to peel Milo off the wall, facing him toward the mirror and standing behind him. A growl escaped as he rested his aching bulge on the crack of Milo's gorgeous ass. *Christ.* That thing was high and tight. The kind of cheeks that would slide up and down his belly like a dream.

If he'd thought Milo was sexy in jeans, nothing came close to seeing him in the mirror, having his cock stroked, his mouth open wide in a silent moan. The denim had dropped to his knees, creating a sight Renner wouldn't be forgetting any time soon. Thighs that hadn't been developed in a gym, but rather doing an honest man's work. There was sinew and cut sections of muscle that contracted with every pump of Renner's fist. His balls were high, just like his ass, swaying front to back as he thrust into the grip Renner continued to tighten.

"*Don't stop, don't stop,*" Milo begged through clenched teeth. With a clumsy hand, he grabbed the red T-shirt and held it up near his throat, giving both of them a better view of his cut-up body. His dick being jacked. "Oh God…the way you're…"

"Tighter grip than you're used to, isn't it?" Renner breathed in his ear. "Have you been beating off the way you *think* it's supposed to be done? Or the way you *need* it to be done?"

"*Fuck.*" Milo swayed, his free hand shooting out to balance him on the wall. "I don't know. I don't know."

Renner was actually, *actually* forgetting himself here. He hadn't thought that was possible, but the lack of control was happening. Milo was leaning back against his chest, tilting his hips up and fucking into Renner's fist. The sounds coming from him were unfiltered and perfect. And God, a natural disaster couldn't have stopped him from dry humping Milo's ridiculous backside, grunting into his shoulder with every thrust like it was *his* first time with a man, too.

It *wasn't*, though. He needed to remember he was the one taking the lead.

The reminder that he was in charge, combined with Milo's pleasure literally resting in the palm of his hand, set off a series of detonations inside Renner's chest. *Possessiveness* chiefly among them. Which was lunacy. Completely out of character. But there it was. So maybe what came next was his decent half trying to scare Milo off…or maybe it was revealing an important part of himself and hoping Milo stayed. For more?

"You don't know how you need it done?" Renner gave him a particularly rough stroke, and Milo jerked against him, precome beading on the tip of his cock. *Perfect. Christ, too perfect.* "There we go. I think we know now, don't we?"

"Yes," Milo pushed through stiff lips. "*Again.*"

"Soon." Renner used his forehead to wrestle into the crook of Milo's neck, scraping his teeth all the way up to his ear. "I make the decisions. Do you understand? Boss inside work, boss outside of work. That's me. Your dick seems to like that idea just fine."

Chapter Eight

Milo couldn't breathe. He couldn't *breathe*. Everything was moving so fast. It moved fast with women, too, but he had practice in that arena. None here. None at all.

Oh, he knew Renner was giving him the best goddamn hand job of his life. No lie. The man had a grip like King Kong on a bad day, and everything—*everything*—was in bright Technicolor because there was a man doing this thing to him. A powerful one. One he'd had filthy thoughts about. The sensations were blunter, more…intense. The stubble from Renner's chin, the deep gravel of his voice, and yes, the kung-fu grip. All reminders that he was being touched by a man. *A man*. Something he'd always wanted in some far-back, repressed part of his being, until he'd realized what he was doing. Hiding.

There was no hiding now, though. This was *happening*, and he was watching it in a mirror, in addition to feeling every incredible pull of his ready-to-pop cock. Curse words bubbled and flowed from his lips, like a filthy poem that made no sense. And maybe he shouldn't be, but he was depending on Renner to translate. Everything.

Renner wasn't giving him time to catch up, though. Milo was still back on first base trying to read the coach's signals, and dude was yelling for him to round home. He wanted to cross home plate. Really fucking bad. He just had to catch up. *Catch up.*

I make the decisions. Boss inside work, boss outside of work.

And yeah…there it was again. His abdomen heaved out at the memory of those words. The same twining, spiking heat he'd experienced when Renner shoved him up onto the desk. What did it mean about him that he got excited by the prospect of being ordered around? Was he flat-out going to like *anything* with a man because he'd been anticipating it for so long? Renner wasn't giving him time to think about it, but pride prevented him from asking for a time-out. Or a slowdown. Wasn't even sure he *wanted* to slow down.

"I like that," he blurted. "I think I like it."

Renner's five-o'clock-shadowed chin nudged aside his shirt collar, rubbing, abrading, and the friction sent more heaviness dropping low in Milo's stomach. "You think you like what?"

"You. Being an asshole." He trapped a groan in his throat when his balls drew up, up. *Jesus,* how far could they go? "You know, to a d-degree." The hand stroking his dick slowed, the clutching digits loosening, and Milo shook his head. "No, no. Keep *going.* More."

He watched wariness battle with fevered interest—*a lot* of it—on Renner's face. "More?" In a surge, he pushed Milo's front up against the mirror. "Haven't had enough yet, have you? Maybe you're a little too brave for your own good."

"Shut up," Milo whispered, starting to shake when Renner picked up the hand job where he'd left off, all rough and firm and *God.* "I'm trying here."

"It shouldn't be a try." Some of the lust in Renner's eyes cleared. "Maybe it wouldn't be so much about trying if it were someone other than me."

That out-of-character admission from the usually confident Renner quickened the pace of Milo's pulse. Big-time. He met eyes with Renner in the mirror and got that big roller-coaster drop feeling, half terrified, half excited. There was a voice in the back of his head saying this was what he'd been waiting for. Some kind of sign the guy was human and now that he knew, every interaction they'd had for months was painted in a different light. Now was really not the time to examine the new insight into Renner's psyche too closely, though, because liquid was dripping from the tip of his cock onto a dressing room floor.

He knew one thing, though. If Renner stopped, this would never happen again.

And despite everything…the idea of this being the last time bothered him. A ton.

"I don't want someone else right now."

"Right…now."

Milo watched his erection slide in and out of Renner's fist, lubricated now by his precome. A sight he'd never expected, but couldn't get enough of. God, even the sound of it was brutally hot. "That's what I said, boss."

Renner growled against the back of his head. "What *do* you want?"

"I thought you were the one who decided what to give me," Milo managed, his teeth starting to chatter. Shit, he wasn't going to last much longer, but a premonition told him there was more. Something amazing. If he just held on and drew Renner back out of his damn head. "So do it."

His final word was cut off when Renner shoved him more solidly against the mirror, his knuckles glancing off the surface as he fucked Milo's brains out with a pumping, demanding hand. "I ought to leave this cock of yours hanging ripe and heavy, shoved back into your jeans, instead of finishing you off. The way you need." Renner's lips raked down his neck, his tongue joining the action to roll Milo's eyes back in his head. "You let me pull your pants down, let me fuck myself up against your pretty-boy ass, and then *challenge* me? You're not ready for what I'd like to give you right now. You won't be ready for a while."

Milo was torn between arousal beyond belief and being all-around pissed. Who the hell did Renner think he was talking to him like that? Telling him what he was ready for? And why could Milo's knees barely hold him up after that speech? Before he could open his mouth and let out whatever decided to emerge, he felt one of the fingers of Renner's free hand…slide down the crease of his ass…then back up.

Every single one of his senses went on red alert, the hair on his arms and neck standing up, his abdomen seizing. He watched in the mirror as Renner stuck that skimming finger into his mouth, drenching it, before dropping it back down to Milo's backside. This time, it slid between his cheeks, slowly, so slowly, and pressed against the rim of his asshole. And he was already choking on oxygen, because just the idea of having a man…*Renner*…touch him there, was a fantasy he'd been locked inside of forever.

"*Relax.*" Renner issued the order in a hard voice that made Milo's muscles tighten on reflex, but he wanted this. *Needed* it. So he breathed through his nose and forced his body to release tension. "Good man. Likes having his dick stroked by a rough hand, but knows he needs more, huh? More than what he's been getting."

"I do," Milo panted. "Please."

His begging ended in a quick intake of breath when Renner's finger started to massage him with tight, no-nonsense drags. Up and down, in circles, the lubrication from his mouth easing the movements. *Fuck.* The *pressure.* It was everywhere. At the bottom of his spine, dead center of his stomach, throbbing in his head. So good. Too good. Milo stared at the mirror through blind eyes, his balls pulling up and getting ready to empty. And when Renner finally pushed his finger inside Milo with a pleased grunt, Milo fell forward, his open mouth pressed against the mirror, fogging it up.

Renner's teeth snapped against the flesh of Milo's neck, leaving a sting. "I'll take care of you on both sides, won't I? The hard *and* the sweet."

Milo slapped his hand against Renner's reflection in response. He couldn't manage words because it was over. Life was *over.* He reached with a blind hand, snatching his security uniform shirt off the seat, coming into the starchy material with a strangled curse. Shit. *Shit.* His stomach was heaving so much, the bottom felt like it had dropped out. As if Renner could read his mind, the grip around his cock turned loose and fast, so *fast,* bringing the need out of him in quick, hot spurts. All the while, the finger that was vying with Renner's hand job to be the center of Milo's universe…it tucked deeper and twisted around, making Milo's body clench involuntarily. But Jesus, that only made the orgasm more brutal. *Fuller.*

"Stop." Milo's balance pitched, his eyes seeking out Renner's to ground him. "Don't stop."

For a brief moment in time, Renner appeared just as stunned as Milo, but he severed the eye contact…way too soon. Pressing his stubbled cheek against Milo's temple, eyelids dropping to conceal the green, he carefully removed his finger and gave Milo's ass a gentle slap. The opposite hand ceased its perfect jerks, holding Milo's satisfied flesh instead, cupping it tightly. Possessively. In a way that almost made Milo hard again. *Wow.* He liked the expression of ownership far too much.

"Do you always come like the world is on fire?"

"No." Milo shook his head, jostling the truth free. "Never."

Renner's gaze flashed, and Milo pretty much watched him disengage from the moment. Like an off switch had been punched. "Well." He stopped touching Milo and stepped back. "Now you know what it takes."

Milo stood with the uniform shirt pressed to his dick as Renner left the room, telling himself feeling abandoned was ridiculous. But unable to stop replaying Renner's words over and over.

Now you know what it takes.

Yeah. Now he knew the *what*.

But he really needed to keep his focus on the *who*.

Travis. Not Renner.

Not Renner.

First and foremost, Renner was his boss, and those rules he'd listed were designed to cross Milo off in three different ways. They didn't even like each other. Not in the traditional way. They were basically sparring partners. Not to mention, Renner would be leaving soon. So had they slipped up here? Or had Renner decided to show him more about his body than what jeans to shove his legs into? Would that kind of... teaching...be a mistake when Milo seemed to crave Renner's aggression?

Yeah. Probably a mistake.

Milo closed his eyes and pictured Travis. Laughing, plating food, talking about the previous night's date. That was more Milo. Fun, easygoing, and light. Not dark, intense, and quick to leave. Taking his eyes off the dressing room door, Milo turned to dress—apparently he *wouldn't* be wearing his uniform shirt—resolve heavy in his mind. He had until the weekend with Renner and his eyes would remain open. No more confusion. If they got physical again, it would be about learning about himself. Not what they could be together.

The whole idea was laughable anyway. Impossible.

"Any day now, Bautista," Renner called, probably checking his watch. "This place is giving me a rash."

Relieved they were back to business as usual, Milo smiled and kicked off his new jeans. "See if they have any bowling shirts in your size. That's where we're headed next."

A gusty sigh. "Don't remind me."

Chapter Nine

Christ. I'm wearing rented shoes.

Renner glanced over at Milo on the bench, and the security guard greeted him with a big, shit-eating grin. But he looked away quickly when the impulse to smile *back* caught him off guard. Yeah. In the history of Renner, today would probably go down as the weirdest.

First of all, yes, he was currently crisscrossing shoelaces that had been tied upward of a thousand times by sweaty, dirty hands, and he was preparing to play a sport where the entire objective was to knock shit down.

Second, this thing with Milo was totally wrong. For many reasons. After the scene in the dressing room, they had somehow slipped right back into their prior mode of behavior. Without a single hitch. At least on the surface. Which made it feel almost like a relationship. Renner had ample experience with men, and he'd come to expect the awkwardness after hooking up. He would ask about the other's plans for the rest of the day, also known as a big hint that those plans would *not* include Renner, and the guy would hit the sidewalk, usually grateful that *he* hadn't been forced to make necessary excuses. Since Renner only saw other businessmen who didn't have time for relationships, nor were they interested in anything beyond sex, this process had become easy. He'd gotten used to it. Perhaps that was why spending time with Milo *after* he'd jerked him off felt…unnatural.

Not that you could tell by the way they continued to bicker at each other, like a married couple who fight-flirted as a method of foreplay.

Not good.

So the third reason this night was weird? He could have easily told Milo where to stuff his rented shoes and gone back to work, where he belonged. But for some insane reason, he *wanted* to stay. He was even willing to suffer through a night with Duke and Vaughn, two men who spoke in a language made up of baseball statistics and home improvement hacks.

Yes, he wanted in on bowling night, because ever since Milo had been hired, Renner had been irritable after hours, wondering where the other man ended up. In bed with someone? *More* than one someones? He'd always pictured women, but now the script had been flipped. Now Renner had this annoying need to make sure Milo went home alone.

In other words, he'd entered an unfamiliar danger zone and didn't have a map to help himself find the fucking exit. That possessiveness he'd encountered back in the dressing room was needling him in the jugular now. Prickling the back of his neck. Not only was it none of his business who Milo took to bed, but he was well aware Milo wanted a *specific* man.

If Renner had thought himself over the past, the skeletons *that* stirred up proved him dead wrong.

"Go ahead," Milo said, dimples popping into view. "I know you want to complain about the shoes."

"The child behind the counter gave me the oldest ones on purpose." Renner stood and rolled his neck. "I can feel myself standing inside several generations of sweat."

"There you go." Milo rose and patted him on the shoulder. "Feel better now?"

"No."

No, he really didn't. Milo's hand was still resting on his shoulder, putting those biceps inches from his mouth. Biceps that were *way* too visible in the red T-shirt Milo had bought and worn out of the store. Why hadn't Renner handed him the next size up, dammit? The material looked like it had been painted on, leaving not a single muscle ridge to the imagination. Worse, Milo had no idea how hot he looked. There was no awareness or overconfidence in his expression, only amusement. Thank God he hadn't worn the jeans out of the store, too, or Renner would be in the bowling alley parking lot, giving the younger man another stroke-off.

Milo's smile had dimmed. "What are you thinking about?"

Your cock. How thick and heavy it felt in my hand. How it jerked and swelled when the come shot out. How you said my name when I pushed my finger where you've never had one before.

"I'm thinking we should have bought you two of those jackets." Renner turned and walked toward the lane where he could hear his brother-in-law Duke's booming voice. "You never know when you'll need a backup. And the price was right."

"I hate that jacket," Milo muttered. "It looks like it was stolen from a child's race car costume."

Renner subdued his smile. "No. It's clearly a seventies television detective costume."

Milo tried to knock him off balance with a shoulder. "Why did you let me buy it?"

"I'm kidding." Milo paused at the top of the carpeted stairs. "It looks fine."

Why was he lying about something so trivial as a jacket? Did he subconsciously put Milo in an ugly jacket to repel men?

Yeah, he had. *Great.*

The bowling alley was bursting with the sounds of laughter, pins being scattered, beer pitchers being slammed down. And the ever-present sounds of men insulting each other formed a layer over everything. Basically, it was the Third Shift with bowling balls.

Duke turned in the scorekeeper's seat, one hand massaging his bad knee. He saw Milo and nodded in greeting, but the action froze when he saw Renner. His brother-in-law recovered fast, however, standing to shake his hand. Whatever differences he'd had with Renner in the past had been eclipsed by Duke's respect for Samantha, Renner's stepsister. Not to mention the ability to forgive that Renner both admired and couldn't stand. It only reminded him he'd been a meddling asshole.

"I see we have a ringer tonight," Duke rumbled. "Surprised they got you in the shoes."

"It wasn't easy," Milo said, skirting past him down the steps and giving Renner no choice but to follow. "We'll put up the bumpers for your turn, boss man."

"That won't be necessary." Renner sat in a bucket seat and scanned their immediate area for anyone checking out Milo. "I'm sure I can manage to roll a ball in a straight line."

"Aw, shit." Vaughn jumped up from where he'd been lounging in one of the chairs opposite Renner. He slapped Milo on the back and gave a respectful nod in Renner's direction. "I sense a competitor's spirit. And a smart man never underestimates beginner's luck, either. Right, Duke?"

The hulking mechanic rolled his eyes. "Go ahead and tell the story. You won't shut up until you do."

Vaughn was already positioning himself, gesturing hands at the ready. "Samantha rolled a two-twenty on her first game a few weeks ago."

Milo paused in the act of choosing his ball. "Get the hell

out of here. Where was I?"

"It was couples' night. We spared you. You're welcome."
Vaughn resumed the story. "So, there's Duke, hovering over the
little wife, explaining the basics like she's twelve. And she's just
smiling away, the way River does when *I'm* mansplaining—"

"We banned that word," Duke interjected. "That word is
banned."

"Whatever," Vaughn said. "Samantha rolls a strike on her
first try and skips—*skips*—back to Duke and lays a big old
smacker on his cheek. Meanwhile, me and River had to leave
the immediate area we were laughing so hard."

"Yeah, well..." Duke punched some buttons on the score
machine. "Samantha got mad at you for laughing and spent
the night making me feel better. So. Joke's on you."

"I really didn't need to know that," Renner muttered.
"Please keep your marital rituals with my sister to yourself."
When Duke only smiled, like a man so content he couldn't
even bother hiding it, Renner added, "Although I don't mind
hearing about her kicking your ass."

Duke's smile grew wider. "Now there's a shock."

Milo fell into the chair beside Renner, bowling ball in
his lap. "While we're on the subject of potentially shocking
things..." His right leg started to bounce. "I'm gay."

Neither man moved. Except for their jaws, which seemed
to unhinge. Actually make that three jaws, because someone
could have sailed a ship through Renner's mouth, too. And
he'd already *known*. He'd just never expected Milo to come
out to his friends with so...little fanfare. Nor did he expect to
have the privilege of being there when it happened.

"I'm not making light of it," Milo continued, his leg now
moving in overtime. Fast enough that Renner had no choice
but to reach over and lay a hand on Milo's knee to stop the
nervous action. Milo looked down and over at Renner—
along with everyone else, though—so he retrieved his hand

and forced himself to look bored. "I'm not saying it should be this easy for everyone. To say the words. But I'm making it easy for me, because it was hard enough for long enough keeping it in. All right?"

Pride. It jammed in Renner's throat like a hockey puck. This man was growing more incredible by the moment in his utter refusal to be...in...now that he was out. He wanted to experience everything in the open and didn't care who knew. Renner had been quick to let everyone in his life know about his sexuality, but he'd been defensive from the word go, almost hoping someone would react negatively. So he could leave that person behind. If that didn't reiterate the differences between himself and Milo, nothing would.

"Well, congrats, man." Vaughn pressed a button on the scorekeeper to call a waitress. "I guess this calls for a toast."

"Samantha already knew," Duke said, pulling off bored way better than Renner. "About you two."

"Wait. Whoa." Renner shook his head, mostly to dislodge the stupid flare of pleasure that someone had thought them a couple. "There's no 'you two.'"

Duke shrugged. "Whoops."

Renner could feel Milo looking at him, but didn't turn his head. Because what would he see? Embarrassment over being linked to him? Thoughtfulness, instead? Neither one would be good. *He wants someone else. You've been here before.* "Listen, let's get this game started before the DNA in these shoes brings them to life and eats us alive." Renner stood. "And I know this is probably the gayest bowling team in history, but if anyone cracks a balls joke, I'm leaving."

Vaughn saluted him. "Fair enough."

Feeling Milo's gaze on his back, Renner went to go search for his own ball among the small leftover selection. On the way, the phone in his pocket vibrated with an incoming email.

He shouldn't have checked it.

Chapter Ten

Milo spun the bowling ball against his palm and watched Renner's back stiffen. To be fair, it was usually stiff over something. Those hockey goaltender shoulders would tighten up, shifting his suit jacket. Only tonight he wasn't wearing the jacket, giving Milo a nice view of what hid beneath. It reminded Milo of a documentary he'd watched once about the continental shift, when huge masses of land had broken off and relocated. That is what the muscles moving under Renner's dress shirt reminded him of. Shifting land mass.

What would they feel like under his tongue?

An image of himself seated on Renner's ass, leaning forward to massage away the tension unfurled in his mind... and his blood rushed south. Wow. He'd just had the hand job of a lifetime less than an hour ago and already his cock was *aching*. Not typical at all. Except for the short time he'd dated Holly Burbank, he used to go months without women.

If the image were real and he were sitting on Renner's backside, would they be naked? Hell yeah. Still wet from a shower so his dick would easily slide up and down the curves of Renner's ass. Could he come like that? Milo thought so. Hell, he was close just thinking about it. How he would use Renner's ass cheeks to stroke himself off. God, maybe Renner would growl an order over his shoulder for Milo to go faster. Until he'd be pumping and panting, his thighs aching from the effort.

And then Renner would flip him over onto his stomach and...

Shit. Milo grabbed his bottle of beer off the score machine and swigged the cold liquid, forcing himself to calm down. Usually, when he witnessed Renner's stress manifest itself, he would make a crack about him being a workaholic. Or tell him to switch to decaf. But now he knew it was more serious. If Renner stayed true to form, he would probably burn rubber back to the factory to fix everything. Now. Tonight.

Hard as it was to admit, Milo needed Renner to stay. Yeah, he knew how selfish that sounded, but he'd just kicked down the closet door. While his friends were being as awesome as he'd hoped they would, Renner had been the steady presence while it was going on. Still was. Maybe he'd underestimated how quickly it would start to feel okay for his friends to know? He was seriously feeling a little exposed here.

"Everything okay?" Vaughn called, walking back from taking his turn. "Or do we need to confiscate the boss's cell phone?"

Milo laughed but it sounded forced to his own ears. "Yeah, maybe."

Before the words were even out of his mouth, Renner was walking up the stairs, giving them the international signal for, *sorry, I need to take this.* And when Renner paused at the front counter to trade back in the bowling shoes for his wing tips, a misshapen anvil sank in Milo's stomach. He didn't know what was bothering him more. The fact that he could miss this chance to hold up his end of the bargain and force Renner to relax? Or being alone with his friends after basically peeling off a layer of skin? Which was ridiculous. Duke and Vaughn were already cracking jokes about each other's bowling techniques and kicking around ideas for Vaughn's new house. They weren't acting any differently around him. It was just... Milo who felt different.

"Hey," Duke called, lumbering back to the score machine and dropping into the chair. "You're up, Bautista."

"Right." Milo scratched the back of his neck, watching as Renner disappeared through the bowling alley exit. "I think I need to go make sure the boss man doesn't try to skip out on us."

"Go ahead." Vaughn and Duke were clearly trying their best to keep speculation out of their expressions. It was almost comical how hard they tried, making Milo like them even more. "We'll take your turns," Duke said. "You can jump right in when you get back."

"Great." Milo headed for the stairs, but stopped and turned when he was only halfway. "Hey, thanks for not being dicks."

Duke and Vaughn threw him an identical salute.

Milo continued on his way through the bowling alley, recognizing more than half of the people in attendance as factory workers, or Hook residents he knew from frequenting the same stores and restaurants. It was kind of crazy how he'd started to belong in such a short space of time. Boston had always been his home, but when Vaughn had called and offered him the security job, he'd realized he'd been missing his army buddies. Guarding and dating a pop star had been interesting at first, until it turned tedious...and the confusion and guilt over wanting Travis had begun to set in. Coming to Hook for a while had been a good decision all around.

But now that he was no longer confused about Travis... would he go back to Boston permanently? What if he went down there for the visit this weekend, revealed the feelings he'd been harboring, and things actually worked out? Excitement trickled into his blood.

Not as much as usual, though, and the excitement had changed. It was less about sex and more about appreciation. Relief. The period he'd known Travis represented Milo's recognizing who he'd been inside all along.

Milo pushed out of the building into the crisp night air, his heart picking up speed when he spied Renner at the rear of the parking lot. Why couldn't the man keep to well-lit areas? Didn't he realize his obvious wealth made him a target? Apparently he hadn't learned a damn thing from the near-mugging. It would serve him right to get jumped again.

Chewing on his lower lip, Milo paced the concrete landing, growing more and more anxious as Renner moved far enough away that his voice began to fade.

"Shit," Milo said under his breath, descending the stairs and striding in Renner's direction. He passed two cars with fogged-up windows, one of them rocking rather violently, before finally reaching his boss. Renner didn't see him at first, though, and Milo hung back, his brown furrowing at the other man's tone. He sounded irritated, as usual. But there was a note of resignation Milo would never have associated with Renner in a million years.

"It was airtight. They should have accepted it." His boss paced, yanking at the collar around his neck. "I can't make the cost of production any lower without it eating into profits and pissing off investors..." He cursed. "Yes, I know that's why the proposal was rejected. I can't exactly do anything about it, can I?" A pause. "I realize this contract would have funded the other Jersey project. I *realize* that, dammit."

Milo shuffled closer without thinking. His intent was to knock the goddamn cell phone out of Renner's hand before the man had a heart attack. Whatever the conversation was about, it had caused Renner to look disheveled in record time. His tie was sideways; his hair had lost its perfect style. And Milo really didn't like it.

Renner's head whipped around at Milo's approach, his annoyance only amplifying. Whoever was on the other end of the line had raised their voice and Milo didn't think, he simply reached for the cell, intending to tell the guy to eat shit, but Renner pulled it out of his reach at the last second. "I'll call you back," he barked into the cell, then hung up. "What the hell do you think you're doing?"

Good question. Was he overstepping his bounds? Yes. Yesterday, he wouldn't have been this ballsy. Maybe when a man jerked you off in a dressing room, you stopped giving a shit about propriety. "Who is that?"

Renner did a double take, as if to say, can you *believe* this guy? "Hudson. My business partner." He stowed the cell in his front pocket. "Not that it's any of your business."

"I beg to differ. My end of the bargain was to show you how to relax." Milo gestured in the general direction of Renner's pocket. "That was having the opposite effect."

His boss regarded him through narrowed eyes. "So... what? I just stop *working* because you decided to make me a part of your little experiment?"

Hurt struck Milo, and he fell back a step. "Experiment?"

"I didn't mean that." Renner dragged a hand down his face. "Jesus, I didn't mean that, all right? I'm in the middle of a work crisis and you don't...*this* doesn't fit into the picture."

"Too bad." Man, his balls were made of solid brass tonight. But it was either go back inside and brood into a beer because Renner had called his major life event an *experiment*, or he could push the guy into admitting why he was trying to deflect. Because that's what was happening. Maybe that was what had been happening all along. Renner treated everyone like garbage so they wouldn't look too closely and see he wasn't perfect after all.

"Did you just say 'too bad'?" Renner took a few steps closer, his head tilted in that condescending way. "This is where I remind you I sign your paycheck, Bautista."

Burn. "There. You played the card. Now we can move on."

Renner laughed without humor. "I sign *everyone's* check. In order to do that, my job can't end at five o'clock. Bad news comes in at all hours, whenever it feels like it."

There it was. With some pushing, he was in. Meager though the information was, he'd never gotten anything significant out of Renner. Until now. "Bad news. Is that what the phone call was about?"

"You tell me," Renner near-shouted. "You were standing there listening the whole time like a nosy washwoman."

"You knew I was there." The realization dawned on Milo slowly. "You wanted me to hear it."

Renner scoffed and yanked the phone back out of his pocket, that big thumb scrolling so fast it was a blur. "You're hilarious."

Milo swallowed and eliminated the distance between them, noticing the way Renner's thumb slowed down. And slowed further. Milo lifted a hand and closed it over the phone, surprised when Renner didn't protest. Didn't look at him, either, but they were fighting one battle at a time. "Tell me about the bad news."

A muscle slid up and down in Renner's throat. "No."

"If you get it off your chest," Milo said, "maybe you can come back inside and forget about it for a while."

"Forget it how? By being surrounded by the countless employees I failed?" The stress was back, putting strain around Renner's mouth and eyes. "There is exactly zero chance of that."

"Failed?" Never expecting his pragmatic boss to admit

something so extreme. And *wrong*. Milo shook his head. "What are you talking about?"

"Look." Renner replaced the phone in his pocket once more, but Milo could hear it buzzing. "Go back inside and enjoy your night. You can harass me about my caffeine intake bright and early tomorrow morning."

Milo was losing him. Losing his chance to see what lay underneath this hard man's exterior. Maybe he'd already lost it. But giving him *some* kind of relief was suddenly so important, Milo was balancing on the balls of his feet. Renner wasn't going to make the move, like he'd done back in the store, and frankly, Milo had grown accustomed to the woman being the aggressor. Neither was happening in this case, though. Not with Renner's mind traveling further and further away. His own initiative was required, but that meant he could be rejected. And the fabric of his new reality was still so fragile, he worried a refusal might tear it straight down the center.

No guts, no glory, though. If coming out to his friends hadn't solidified that belief, nothing would. Milo ran his sweaty palms down the legs of his jeans, then lifted his right hand, curling it in the front of Renner's dress shirt. The wind seemed to stop blowing while Milo's heart thudded in his throat. Although the boss's eyes were narrowed to slits, he allowed Milo to pull him closer. Closer. Until they were breathing right up against each other's mouth.

"Getting brave, are you?" Renner murmured.

God. A single graze of their lips and Milo's cock was already at half mast. "Maybe. Yeah."

Renner nodded down at Milo's fisted hand. "I told you I'm the one who decides when this happens. And how."

"Well, you were taking too fucking long." A flash of something blew through Renner's expression. Like a cross between arousal and affection, but Milo might have imagined the second part. "I figured since you refuse to talk to me, I could find another way to chill you out."

"And you think touching you is going to accomplish that?" Renner untangled Milo's hand from his shirt and pressed it firmly up against his fly. *Sweet Christ.* Milo was winded at a moment's notice, his lungs gathering oxygen in huge pulls. He was touching Renner's dick. It was the first man he'd touched like this *at all*, which was crazy all by itself. But the thick curve of it...the sturdy root...felt so insanely good in his hand, he had to squeeze. To rake his palm up and down. And there was no more satisfying sound than his experienced boss gritting a shaky curse. "That feel chilled out to you? In any way?"

"No." Milo swallowed a protest when Renner circled his wrist and tugged it away. *Don't sound desperate. Don't sound desperate.* "Why don't we try for taking your mind off the phone call instead?"

Their faces were only a breath apart, but he could still see Renner's eyes light with challenge. "Let's see what you got."

Milo might have lost his nerve if it weren't for the note of need in that dare. And hell, hadn't he just felt undeniable proof in his hand? He wasn't the only hungry one here. "All right, boss man." He walked Renner backward until his back hit the chain-link fence marking the perimeter of the parking lot. "You asked for it."

Their hard cocks wedged together between dipping and shuddering stomachs. Milo couldn't stop himself from giving a hard roll of his hips, listening to the answering drag of the fence on the asphalt, Renner's bit-off groan. On one side of them, freeway traffic rushed by in the distance. On the other, car doors slammed and bowling alley patrons laughed their way up and down the steps leading inside. But their racing breath drowned everything else out after a few seconds, becoming the only thing Milo could hear.

"You don't seem very worried about being caught,"

Renner murmured, his gaze locked on Milo's mouth. "I wish you would stop surprising me."

"Yeah?" He hooked his fingers in Renner's belt loops and ground their lower bodies together. "Sorry to inform you that ain't happening tonight."

And then he just went for it.

Shit, it was glorious.

Renner clearly didn't know what hit him when the kiss started, making Milo's mouth curve as it slanted over his first set of hard, male lips. Milo could kiss like nobody's fucking business—true fact. It was one thing in his life that he was a little arrogant about. When he'd dated Holly, she'd gotten drunk and laid one on him, right before passing out in the backseat of her tinted black SUV. The following morning, she'd had no recollection of anything from the previous evening. Except for the kiss. She'd asked Milo out on a date and promptly begged for another.

At the moment, however, the pop star was the *furthest* thing from Milo's mind, because Renner was no slump in the kiss department, either. In fact, his initial shock had passed and now…oh God, the boss man had beat him to introducing tongue action. *Damn,* he was smooth with it, too. A lot like he'd stroked Milo's cock earlier, he didn't take any prisoners. The stubble was a new sensation for Milo, and he wanted more, wanted closer, and Renner gave it to him. He sank his fingers into Milo's hair and angled his head, delivering sweeping drives of his tongue, abrasive brushes of his chin and cheeks.

Just as Milo was beginning to run out of breath, Renner switched their positions, not being the least bit gentle about throwing Milo up against the chain-link fence. "Was that you *smiling* while you kissed me, pretty boy?" He brought their foreheads together, catching Milo's lower lip and holding it while he growled. "There's nothing funny about how bad I want to lay you across one of these car hoods and yank your tight work pants down."

"They're not that tight," Milo blurted, because he couldn't think of anything else to say. Not when his aching dick was meshed with Renner's and the man was talking about doing a hell of a lot more than they'd done in the dressing room. Not when every worry for the future had dwindled into nothing except the man in front of him. His commanding voice had become the only thing that moved him.

"They *are* that tight. Believe me." Renner's hands were rough, demanding as they wedged between Milo and the chain-link fence to knead his ass. *Hard.* "Not as tight as this would be, though. Isn't that right?"

Milo couldn't respond, because Renner snared his mouth in a second kiss. More exploring this time. Like he was trying to find out the answer to a question, but neither of them seemed to know what it was. Renner's grip on his ass was insistent, keeping his hips angled forward as they struggled to drag their erections side to side, up and down, through two sets of pants. Jesus, had he really wondered if he could come by sliding his naked cock against Renner? He might orgasm just like this. Rubbing their bulging flies together. *Amazing*.

He was craving more words, more reassurances from Renner, and the man obliged, breaking the mind-blowing kiss to speak harshly at Milo's lips. "Are you thinking of yourself beneath me on the hood of one of these cars yet?" His breath rushed in Milo's ear, sending a hot shiver down to his tightening spine. "Maybe you'd like me to pick one close to the entrance, so everyone could watch me rock into you for the first time."

The image was so startlingly hot, so unexpected, Milo almost lost his load, right there in his pants. "Is that…the kind of thing you like?"

"I'd like anything that included fucking you," he rasped

into Milo's ear, thrusting them up against the fence. "You'd draw quite a crowd, wouldn't you? A tight pretty boy getting it for the first time from his boss." His mouth pushed into Milo's neck, followed by a scrape of teeth. "You think you'll scream my name? Or Travis's?"

Cold. Milo went cold everywhere. His stomach, the dead center of his chest. One second, he couldn't have been more certain that he was going to flood his briefs. The next, he couldn't get out from between Renner and the chain-link fence fast enough. He shoved at Renner's big shoulders—hard. "Get *off* me."

Renner stared at the spot where Milo had been, propping his hands on his hips, chest heaving with labored breaths. "It just slipped out."

"Yeah? Well…"

What was Milo mad about? Wasn't this whole arrangement with Renner meant to prepare him to approach Travis? So they'd taken it a step further, but that didn't change what they'd agreed upon at the outset. Just because it had seemed more about them being in a moment together than…someone else being in future moments…didn't mean anything.

Or did it?

"I was just surprised, all right? I mean, maybe I'm not the only one who needs to tighten up my game." His laugh sounded unnatural, tinny. "Bringing up another person while kissing is almost never a good idea."

Even though his imminent need for relief had passed, his cock responded to the sight of Renner adjusting his bulge, re-tucking his shirt into his pants. But the resurgence of lust dimmed when the bastard took out his cell phone, which was lighting up like a blinking Broadway sign. "I have to admit, you took my mind off things for a while." He cleared his throat and headed for the parking lot. "Back to reality now, though. Please make my excuses to your friends." There was a hitch in his stride and he slowed to a stop. "Please let me know one of them drove you home safely?"

What *was* this thing between them? Milo's irritation over Renner's pulling a quick exit was put on hold, all because the man showed concern for his safety. He didn't have an explanation, either. Only knew it caused something to twist in his stomach. "Listen, can you stay? Can we just forget you said something stupid?" Milo took a step toward Renner, but the other man backed up. "If anyone should be pissed, it's me, you know."

"Yeah, I do know." Renner shook his head. "So why would you want me to stay?"

"Because I'm kind of getting used to having you around." He'd never felt more inadequate in his life, standing in front of this man with all the answers, with his identity so firmly in hand, and attempting to convince him they could make a difference for each other. Maybe Milo *couldn't* realistically offer him that. "I don't know. I guess I thought we were becoming friends."

Something about what Milo said seemed to strike a chord. But not the right one. "I don't have time for friends." Renner turned on a heel, his long strides eating up the asphalt on the way to his Mercedes. "Please let me know you have a ride home. Good night."

Chapter Eleven

Today was a new day.

Last night had been just the kick in the ass Renner had needed. Christ, not only was he wallowing in self-pity over losing the Rocky Mountain Ltd. account to a competitor, but he'd let this thing with Milo and Travis get under his skin. Not anymore.

Renner hit send on an email and leaned back in his chair, hearing the lunchtime bell go off on the factory floor below. He'd already done a full day's work and it was only noon. It was amazing what he could accomplish when he stopped mooning over some guy seven years his junior and put his focus where it needed to be. On growing the company.

Last night's reality check was still fresh, but he was ignoring it. Right. He definitely wasn't thinking about the way Milo had flinched when he'd said the other man's name. Wasn't thinking about how *consumed* he'd been by the kiss until he'd fucked it up. And he certainly wasn't thinking about how the person he'd begun feeling undeniably possessive over wanted someone else. Yes, that's where the work came in to distract him. Proposals and emails and purchase orders and investment strategies.

Along with this fresh perspective, he'd also woken up with a handle on this...thing with Milo. There had been a period of his life spent feeling bad for himself—and he wasn't going back to that place. So he would do what he did best. Tidy up loose ends and move on. Milo was closer than he realized to owning his sexuality; he simply needed a push. Renner would provide it. Then he'd make for the exit, much like he'd done last night. Without looking back.

Renner had just decided to skip lunch and plow through another round of emails when he heard the familiar tread coming up the metal stairs to the second floor. When his door opened a moment later—without a knock, of course— Renner's fingers stuttered on the keyboard, but he didn't look up from his computer. "The door is closed for a reason."

"There's a lunch break for a reason," Milo returned, even more annoyance in his tone than usual. "You're going to eat this sandwich if I have to feed it to you myself."

Languid heat melted in Renner's stomach over the prospect, making him grimace. "Leave it on my desk. I'm busy."

"No way." Milo's work boots bumped into his desk. *Thump.* "It'll sprout mold by the time you get around to eating it."

"You're such a nag."

"I know. I'm such a dick, bringing you lunch, aren't I?" Milo slumped into the chair opposite Renner's desk and waited until Renner stop typing and turned. "I bet you're wondering what you need to say to get rid of me, aren't you?"

It had crossed his mind. People were usually pretty easy to lose once they started to get close enough to count his flaws. Why did *this* man continue to persist? All things considered, he'd been worse to Milo than almost anyone. Apart from that hand job.

Milo started to tick off his fingers. "I mean, you told me you don't want me as a friend—"

"That's not true. I told you I didn't have *time* for friends."

"I was the only one standing there, so it's the same thing." Milo didn't wait for him to respond. "You've reminded me on more than one occasion that you sign my paycheck. And if we counted dismissive looks as comments, there'd be at least fifty *fuck offs* to add to this list."

None of this was sitting well. It was like someone was dragging a hot iron across his chest. "Is there a point to this practiced speech?"

"Yeah." Milo leaned forward, hands linked loosely between his knees. "I'm not going away. That's the point."

The hope flapping its wings in his throat was atrocious. He resented it. Didn't want it. "Yes, but *I'm* going away."

"I know." A heavy shadow slipped across Milo's expression. "I might go away, too. From Hook. Depending on what...happens." He meant with Travis. God, he was talking about some guy who cooked and smiled and probably possessed wide-eyed optimism. Like Milo. *Not* like Renner. That didn't stop him wanting to shout *I kissed you last night. That was* me. "But if we both stayed here, working in this factory for another couple decades," Milo continued, "I would keep climbing the stairs and annoying you like this. If things stayed the same, I wouldn't go away or give up on being your friend. Because you deserve to have one. So technically, even if we both go away...*I'm* not. I'm refusing." Milo shoved to his feet and adjusted his security belt. "So eat your fucking sandwich."

Oh, great. The guy was just going to waltz into his office and drop a bomb on him, then leave? It was infuriating. He'd given no real reason for Milo to want to be his friend, and yet he remained steadfast. Delivering sandwiches and trying to make him relax. Renner watched the younger man walk to the office door, the lump in his throat multiplying and growing horns. "Wait." Milo stopped and half turned. "If you would stop trying to win a humanitarian award for five seconds, I would tell you about tonight."

"Tonight?"

"Yes." Renner rose from the desk chair, smoothing a hand down the front of his shirt. Milo's gaze tracked the movement, making Renner think of the previous night's kiss, but he commanded himself to focus. "You asked for my help, so I'm giving it." He tried to clear the sludge from his lungs, but it remained. "You told me this Travis likes to go out, so — "

"You're. Taking *me* out?"

Renner was momentarily speechless over the way Milo's face transformed. Like blinds opening in front of a sunny window. "Yes." He held up a finger when Milo started to interrupt again. "But please stop acting like a nightclub is Mars, for the love of God. You could *easily* do this on your own, but apparently you're rubbing off on me because I feel..." He shivered. "Obligated to guide your path. You've turned me into gay Yoda. It's not a good look."

Milo's lips twitched. "Actually, I think it's your best look."

"What do you know?" Renner flicked a hand at him. "You bought a seventies detective jacket."

"It's a race car costume, and you *made* me buy it."

Renner shrugged, mostly to hide the laugh he was battling to keep inside, but his hip shifted a file on his desk. *The* file. The one he'd been staunchly ignoring all morning in favor of looking ahead and not back. A feat that was easier said than done, now that he'd stopped working furiously. He gave the file a look of distaste and shoved it into the file cabinet behind him. "Let's try to leave Hook around eight. We'll probably hit some traffic into Manhattan — "

Milo was suddenly standing behind him. "What was

that?" He tried to pry open the file cabinet, but Renner snagged his wrist, unable to ignore the way the younger man's pulse jumped. "I'm a trained observer, you know. That's the same file you were frowning about yesterday."

"Enough, Milo," he said, wearily. "I don't want to talk about it."

"You called me Milo. Not Bautista." He raked his teeth over his bottom lip, and Renner's dick practically groaned. "That's progress, Yoda."

"Get out of my office and I'll eat the damn sandwich." *Don't leave.*

"Come on." Milo took back his wrist and hopped up onto Renner's desk. "It's the same thing you were arguing about on that phone call, isn't it? What's up?"

"I lost an account, all right?" Renner blurted. "Technically, I never even had it. But they turned down our proposal. End of story." When Milo only stared at him thoughtfully, Renner pushed an irritated hand through his hair. "What?"

"Nothing, I..." Milo's gaze cut in the direction of the factory floor. "I guess I never considered you might take losses along with the wins. You seem so in control of everything."

Discomfort crept into Renner's throat. "I am. This wasn't something I could control." He stood and paced away from the desk, looking out at the employees filing outside or into the break room. "Samantha and Duke have helped put more of a family-friendly face on Bastion Enterprises, but this particular *massive* account...they're still not interested."

Silence passed. "Family-friendly." He heard a creak and knew Milo was off the desk. Coming toward him? "They won't give you the account because of who you are."

"Yeah." Renner tried to sound flippant, but didn't pull it off. "But every time they release a new product and put out feelers for a United States-based manufacturer to complete the orders, I submit a proposal. It's consistently better than my competitors' offerings, but they persist in rejecting it. Me." He felt Milo behind him and forced himself not to turn. Any kind of sympathy would only make the disappointment worse. The man had just admitted he thought Renner was all but invincible—he didn't need to witness the letdown. "Really, I should have stopped giving a shit a long time ago. The corporation is strong without the account. I don't *need* their approval."

"But you want it?"

"I don't know. I don't *know* what it's really about." He tapped a knuckle against the glass, the *ding* resonating in his head. Milo's silhouette came into focus behind him and the words just flowed. Flowed right out like water, in a way he'd never experienced with another person. "Maybe it's about winning. Or proving I can operate in any world. Any circle. There have been people along the way who didn't think I could. Whatever the reason…I'm done. I'm not trying anymore. It's not worth the added stress."

Milo was silent so long, Renner was finally compelled to turn and witness the disappointment on the other man's face firsthand.

But Milo wasn't disappointed. He was pissed.

"Fuck. *That*."

Chapter Twelve

Renner tilted his head at Milo. "Excuse me?"

"I said—"

"Yes, I heard you," Renner replied, sauntering forward, hands clasped behind his back. "*Fuck that*, you said. Was there anything else you wanted to add?"

"Sure is," Milo answered, pulling up his security belt. He just needed to figure out how to articulate this anger jabbing into his sternum like a pointy stick. He was indignant. And he could literally count on one hand the amount of times he'd worked up a good enough head of steam to use that description. Milo kept it light. But he didn't like people screwing with his friends, especially when the reason wasn't even close to fair. Or right.

He'd been working with Renner for months. Watched him more than was probably natural, marveling at how comfortable the guy was in his own skin. He worked longer hours than anyone Milo had encountered in his twenty-six years. After that comment he'd made in the parking lot last night about letting down countless employees, Milo had his number. The boss man cared. He cared and he busted his butt. Meanwhile, unbeknownst to…well, everyone…there were people out there stepping on his neck. Trying to keep him down.

"Okay, I'm ready," Milo said.

"Glad to hear it." Renner nodded. "You have the floor."

Milo blew out a breath. "I wasn't here when you bought the factory, but I've seen the changes. You put in newer, safer machines. You improved working conditions. Made the factory greener…whatever *that* means. People might not like you, but they don't exactly *hate* you, because of those things."

"My heart is full."

"Shut up." Milo shifted in his boots, suddenly a little uncomfortable over having Renner's undivided attention. He had a lot that needed saying, but the boss had a brilliant mind and everything in Milo's head could come out sounding like dog shit. "You're doing a great thing here. I'll probably never see your other factories, but I know the standards you keep, and I'm sure they're just as well operated. So what I'm saying is, this company that didn't want you? It's their loss." When Renner started to interject, he held up a hand. "But I don't think you should give up on them. This is important to you, so figure out a way to win the account."

Renner clearly hadn't been expecting him to say that. Maybe he was onto something?

Or maybe…dog shit?

"I've been listening to you yap on the phone for long enough to learn a few things. So I know there's never only one horse in a race. What is this company's product?"

"Hardware designed for education. Calculators, early-learning computers. Primarily for schools. I was going to cut some of our less lucrative accounts and designate several of the new machines downstairs to completing orders." Stress lines bracketed Renner's mouth as he explained. "It would have meant hiring another two dozen employees and possibly opening another location close enough that people from Hook could commute. It would have been good for the town."

Milo wanted to kiss him so badly in that moment, he had to breathe through the impulse. But it didn't go away. "Who else makes the same products?" Once again, Renner looked surprised by the line of questioning, but managed to rattle off a few names. "Great. Let's pitch *them*. If this other company doesn't want us—even though we're literally the best—we'll make it really easy and cheap for his competitors to use our factories. And why wouldn't the competitors give us their accounts? On top of lowering costs, they're going to get a tax break from the government for using green manufacturing. They would be crazy to turn you down, and guess who'll come looking to make nice?" Milo jerked a thumb at the file cabinet. "Those suckers."

Renner stared at him so long, a drip of sweat rolled down Milo's spine. Okay, maybe he'd gone way out of his league, trying to spitball manufacturing strategies, but at least Renner wasn't laughing at him. Yet.

He'd just decided to drop the whole subject and remind the boss to eat his lunch when Renner came toward him. Not slowly, either. He moved so fast, he knocked Milo off balance, but Renner caught him around the lower back with a steadying arm. It was unbelievable how fast Milo was turned on. *Snap.* Less than two seconds had passed since Renner stormed closer, and by the time their mouths locked together, Milo's cock was the weight of a fucking sandbag, hoisted up against the fly of his pants, nudging Renner's own erection.

Renner's free hand molded to the back of Milo's head, pulling him close, holding him so tightly their teeth grazed each other's lips, before deepening the kiss. *Jesus,* when their tongues got into the action, they both sank, sank, groaning like it had been way too long, when it had only been a matter of hours. And a lot like last night, Milo could feel himself losing the battle with reality right away, his mind zeroing in on the friction of Renner's beard and the possessive quality of his hands. But with his last remaining ounce of clarity, he recognized his need to make it about Renner.

The indignation hadn't gone away. At all. He was still pissed on Renner's behalf. How long had he been going through this shit alone? Now that he knew the gist of the situation, he could piece together the phone call from last night. Enough to know the business partner wasn't exactly supportive. Someone needed to be. Someone needed to remind Renner he was the badass who walked into a factory full of people every day who eye-rolled behind his back — and got the damn job done.

They came up for air, and Milo realized Renner was backing him toward the desk, one hand gripping Milo's hair, the other unhooking his security belt. It was Milo's instinct to let Renner lead, too. He recognized that part of himself and kind of loved it. Not right now, though. He was determined to get Renner right where he wanted him.

"Go sit down," Milo managed through heavy breaths against Renner's mouth.

Clearly planning on ignoring the order, Renner hooked his fingers in Milo's belt loops and tugged him up onto desk — impressive, considering Milo was a big man himself — and moved in, groaning for another kiss, palms sliding up the insides of Milo's thighs.

Going for there. God, he needed touching there. So bad. *Bad.*

But he needed something else more.

Milo eluded Renner's mouth, putting both hands on his shoulders and shoving hard, putting the boss man in one of the meeting chairs facing the desk. For a few heavy breaths, he was torn between needing to take advantage of Renner's surprise…and needing to *look*. Because shit, the man wasn't himself in that moment. He was kind of a mess, his hair fucked up, buttons open halfway down his chest. In the sprawled position, his legs were spread, drawing attention to the bulging ridge at their center.

Renner wiped perspiration off his upper lip with a slow drag of his thumb. "Did you just push me?"

"Yeah." Milo slid off the wooden furniture and finished unhooking the security belt, leaving it on the desk. Then he went down on his knees, nerves tap-dancing in his stomach. "That's right, boss man. I pushed you." He swallowed hard before rubbing a palm over the outline of Renner's hard cock. "I wouldn't recommend reminding me you sign my paycheck right now."

Renner's stomach heaved out, then shuddered back in. "Why is that?"

Bracing his upper arms on Renner's sturdy thighs, he leaned close, licking the seam of Renner's fly, tasting the throb beneath. "Because I might have to stop. And I'm feeling pretty eager to learn."

"*Fuck.*" Renner's hands slapped down on the armrests, his knuckles turning white. "You *do* have to stop. This is…this isn't even on my rule list because it should never get this far."

Milo unhooked Renner's belt, letting it sag to either side, before lowering his fly. "See, in the manufacturing business, we call that a loophole."

Renner gritted a curse. "You've got a smart mouth, don't you?"

"I think that's what we're trying to find out." A sound wafted down between them. One Milo had never heard before. Renner's laugh. It was rich and bold and smoky. His fingers actually forgot what they were doing for a second, before he resumed the task of lowering Renner's zipper. "You've got a great fucking laugh, you know."

Milo tugged down Renner's briefs and wrapped a fist around the insanely thick root of Renner's cock, bringing his erection out into the open. "You have a great laugh, too," Renner wheezed. Actually *wheezed* because of Milo. "I'm just never the one who makes you do it. Never will be."

"I don't know about that," Milo murmured, barely cognizant of what Renner had said or the importance of it. Later. He would think about it later. Right now, there was a dangerous fear of failure squeezing his gut. He'd never given head to a man before. And he was starting with the top of the food chain. Hadn't his fifth-grade teacher told him to aim high? *Why are you thinking about fifth grade?* "God, you look like you taste so good."

"*Milo.*" Renner's fingers tangled in his hair, urging him to look up. "We shouldn't be doing this. Not here. I—"

Milo licked out with his tongue and circled the head of Renner's dick, bringing a growl out of the other man that poured him full of blistering heat. "I *want* to suck you off right here. I want you to remember me on my knees, my head bobbing up and down between your legs, next time someone tries to fuck around with you. Or tries to make you forget that you run shit." Another, longer lick. "You're the man, Renner. So sit back, watch me make you come, and *feel* like it."

Of course, now that he'd talked a big game, he had to back it up. His nerves weren't building, though, they were calming, because there was simply no room for them. Lust had a stranglehold on his insides, the rock-hard flesh in his fist feeling seven thousand shades of right. He really hadn't imagined the act of getting on his knees as much as he should have, but already Milo knew that was going to change. God yeah. Because as soon as he enfolded the fat head of Renner's cock in his mouth, instinct came roaring to the forefront.

"Shit, go easy," Renner near-shouted above him. "You swallow me whole, this is going to be over way too fast." He tugged on Milo's hair while he shifted in the chair, positioning himself like a king. Leaned back, thighs spread. "I'm going to enjoy that smart mouth more than I have the right to."

Milo didn't want to go slow. He wanted to experience all of it at once and have the mysteries of the universe solved before lunchtime. The taste. *Christ*, the taste. A little salty from the moisture that had beaded at the tip when he'd given that second lick…and Irish Spring soap. Milo racked his brain trying to remember what he liked most during a blow job—besides imagining a man giving it to him—and everything came into smooth focus.

The thickness stretching his lips wider every time he went down, then pulled up nice and slow. He ran a firm thumb along the underside of Renner's cock, gliding it through the slickness his mouth had left behind, flicking his tongue against the tip. And yeah, Renner liked that a lot. Liked being teased a little bit. *Jesus*. Just knowing this big, commanding man wanted to be tortured made Milo's own cock swell in his pants.

"Take it out," Renner rasped. "Take out your dick and jack yourself off for me. But if you stop giving me what I need, I'll make you put it back away. I don't care how pretty it is to look at. You understand?"

Milo nodded, so out of his mind aroused now, he couldn't follow the demand right away. He fisted Renner's cock at the base and hollowed his cheeks out sucking him hard. The other man jerked in the chair, his hips thrusting toward Milo's mouth, broken curses punctuating the air. And that's when Milo went back to slapping the tip with his tongue.

"Shit. Shit. You aren't even talking and that mouth is still being smart, isn't it?" He pulled on Milo's hair until it stung. "I told you to take out your cock."

Milo's groan was shaky as he took Renner halfway to his throat, dropping his hands to his fly to work the button and zipper, his haste making him clumsy. He hummed around the flesh sitting on his tongue and gripped his dick, freeing it from the uniforms pants…and another hint of saltiness coated his tongue.

"That's right. I love that smooth piece of yours." Renner urged Milo's head to suck, tugging it closer to his lap. "Wasn't always your ass I was checking out in those fucking pants, was it? No, I used to go crazy wondering who was taking care of it after hours. It's mine right now, though, so stroke it off like I asked you to. Make us both come hard."

He'd never imagined that beating himself off could be better than sex, but with Renner thick and hot in his mouth, it was like a prolonged orgasm from start to finish. He actually had to stop stroking and apply pressure to his balls more than once to stop from letting loose too soon. *God. Fuck.* Renner's dick was growing in his mouth, his hips starting to shift around like he couldn't sit still, and *those noises*. The noises he was making. Grunts and rushes of breath and gritted moans. They were the best kind of music because it was Milo pleasing him. No one else.

Should he be feeling this level of pride over that?

Was it because it was a man…or because it was Renner?

Renner. *Renner.*

"You need to come a lot faster this time. Faster than it took you in my hand." Renner's big body shuddered beneath his mouth and Milo sucked harder. Took him deeper until his eyes went glassy with reflexive tears and still—still—he wanted more. *All.* "Is that because you've got your throat open for me, wide enough to swallow me whole? You love it so much, your dick can't handle it?" Renner growled, his hips pumping off the chair. "*Fuck.* I'm so hot watching you make up for lost time with my cock. You can't get enough. Just like I can't get enough of that pretty-boy mouth."

Milo needed Renner to know the answer to those

questions, whatever they had been, so he swirled his tongue up to the tip and let the head go with a *pop*. "Yes. Yes. I love it."

"Then stop holding back, goddammit. I want to watch you come." He hissed out a breath and Milo felt the dam start to break inside him. Felt the increased throb of Renner's cock in his mouth and God, he was eager. More eager to taste the flood than set loose his own. "Give yourself a hard jerk, Milo, the way I did it. *Harder*. That's right. Come in your hand and get me the fuck off."

Milo knew his teeth were going to clamp down so he released Renner from his mouth, shouting into the coarse skin of the other man's shaking inner thigh. He could sense the strain, could sense Renner holding on. His huffed half breaths, half moans were the final proof his end was near. As soon as the highest peak of Milo's climax passed, he wrapped his lips around Renner's cock and pulled, using both hands to massage the base in a twisting motion.

And he would fantasize about what happened next for the next fifty years. Renner's big hips arched off the chair and he pulled Milo's mouth tight, tight against his lap. It seemed involuntary, but Milo didn't give a shit. It was incredible. Thickness crowded in his mouth, heat met his constricted throat, and all the while, Renner ground out a roar, his hands like iron on the back of Milo's head. It hurt, it was coming home, it was finally the meaning of sex he'd been looking for, and he never wanted it to end.

Milo didn't realize Renner had released him until he heard his own deep, gulping breaths. Until he felt the tightly woven carpet under his hands and saw he'd fallen backward. He looked up at Renner, more than a little fascinated by the sight of him wincing and putting his still-shiny cock away. "Milo." Renner zipped his pants and leaned forward, swiping away the sweat on his forehead. "I shouldn't have made you take that much at the end. No one should ever handle you like that." His exhales were still shaky. "Especially me. I knew it was your first—"

"Why are you apologizing?" Milo tilted his head to the right and wiped his mouth on the inside of Renner's knee. "That was my favorite part. I loved it."

Renner's forehead gathered like a storm. "You loved it in general? Or with me?"

All movement ceased between them, but inside Milo's chest, the tempo of his hammering heart increased. *Wap wap wap.* He'd been subconsciously asking himself the same question...and he thought he might know the answer now. Maybe he'd suspected it for months and he'd just been waiting for fate to take a hand, because he'd been too green to do it himself. Renner had fascinated him and awed him from day one, but he'd grown to know the man and his habits and gripes...and the good parts, too. Like this moment. His visible concern as he leaned down, his right hand flexing as though it wanted to touch Milo's cheek, but didn't understand the impulse.

That wouldn't make Milo's chest ache unless there was a damn good reason, and he'd learned to follow his instincts. Did putting aside his hopes with Travis make him...flippant, though? The weight pressing down on his lungs didn't feel anything but genuine. Not even a little bit. But maybe he needed more time to examine so he didn't jump into something with Renner...and end up disappointing him.

"I-I think..." Milo gained his feet, Renner's eyes following him like a hawk. "I don't know—"

"Look." Renner stood and moved past him in a blur. "I wasn't really thinking straight. You don't have to..." He laughed, but there was no humor in it this time. None of the rich smoke. Milo died a little bit over the lack. "You don't have to have exclusive feelings for someone to enjoy that," Renner said briskly, nodding back toward the chair where he'd been sitting. "Just forget I asked."

"I don't *want* to forget," Milo said, growing pissed. Mostly at himself for not just following his gut. He'd severed something by balking at a simple question. But he'd given the right answer, hadn't he? Didn't make it any easier watching Renner shut down after making himself vulnerable. Fuck it, Milo was pretty damn exposed himself at the moment, too, after what they'd done. It was a two-way street. "And maybe I *do* need exclusive feelings to enjoy what we did. I'm just not sure yet."

"Well." Renner hit a few keys on his computer, morphing back into work mode. "That's something you need to work out on your own."

Milo's skin drew taut, hot spikes climbing the back of his neck. There it was. Full-fledged pissed-off-ness now. "If you're going to throw me back out on my own after every time something happens between us, then maybe you're working it out *for* me." In desperate need of air and maybe a beer or two, Milo stormed toward the door. Throwing it open, he stopped and gave a sweeping gesture toward the blow job chair, as it would henceforth be known. "And by the way, *you're welcome*, you prick."

He pretended not to hear Renner sighing his name as he slammed the door.

Chapter Thirteen

Renner was a senior in college when he had his heart shattered.

As an adult, he could look back and laugh. There was never a ring of truth to the laughter, however, because the impact had been deep. Deep enough to rearrange the frozen tundra of his emotions. Renner's father was a cold, calculating asshole, but he and Renner had somehow managed to retain a decent relationship. There had been a few years of silence after his father treated Samantha poorly in the divorce from her mother, but they shared business news when they had time. There was a definite strain now, but that was par for the course with two men who rarely delved below another person's surface.

Until Renner had met Kieran, the rowing team captain who would eventually ditch him for a teammate, Renner had been happy with short acquaintances. Usually older men with no affiliation with the university he attended, although there had been *one* ill-advised evening with a professor during sophomore year. The way he'd operated with men had been very similar to how his father dealt with women. Quick and detached.

So he'd been shocked when one night hadn't been enough with Kieran. Shocked and more than a touch apprehensive. How did one proceed in asking for a second date? What would it be like when their appetite for sex wasn't so urgent? Turned out, he didn't have anything to worry about. Or so he'd thought. Renner and Kieran had fallen into a routine of classes, work, nights in the city, mornings in bed, weekends out of town. Renner had even met Kieran's mother.

Renner had bought a ring. Christ, how embarrassing. He'd had a whole proposal worked out. A plan to get married in Vermont. The simple piece of jewelry had been burning a hole in his pocket the night Kieran broke it off. At the same coffee shop where they'd met. While the new boyfriend had waited at a corner table, buried in the shadows.

Fifteen years later, Renner could still remember that sinking feeling he'd had from the moment Kieran walked into the place. How the sensation had grown more and more ugly until he'd been sure he would vomit. And that was before his suspicions were confirmed. After that, the ugliness had just poured out, in the form of backhanded insults and the ruination of every memory they'd created together.

To this day, the ugliness continued to pour out, apparently, if this afternoon with Milo was any sort of proof. Hell, he'd fucked *up*. In more ways than one. First, he'd forgotten the lesson he'd learned in college, letting his guard drop and all but *begging* Milo to burn him. While the reminder had still glowed hot, he'd reverted back to his bad habit of striking back at the other man where it hurt. Thinking of the way Milo had withdrawn, like he'd been cracked in the jaw by a baseball bat, was the reason Renner had been sitting at his kitchen table for an hour without moving. Staring at his car keys.

There was an hour left before he and Milo were scheduled to meet, but Renner didn't hold any delusions that they were still heading to Manhattan together. Actually, he should be packing, so he could drive there alone and not look back, until the business gave him no choice. Why wasn't he moving, then? Could it have something to do with the seasickness that started in his belly and swelled to his head at the very thought of not seeing Milo anymore? Because it was real and it was serious. He'd actually taken a Dramamine.

It wasn't *just* the sex that had him thinking nonstop about Milo. Renner had been able to say that only one other time in his life—and it had ended with an ax falling, severing his neck. But the way Milo had defended him and hell, come up with a pretty goddamn good idea to lock down the Rocky Mountain Ltd. account, is why Renner couldn't seem to rise from the table. To do what needed to be done. Leaving would protect him from the inevitable shitstorm when Milo left to go see Travis. And chose Travis. Because he would. Travis would want Milo, too, because he was fucking incredible.

Renner would be left sitting in the coffee shop with the proverbial ring in his pocket.

A knock on the apartment door interrupted Renner's dread. Hope lit up like a beacon in his stomach at the prospect of Milo coming to see him, although he would give the security guard shit for making the first move, when Renner owed *him* the apology.

Renner forced down the fist lodged in his throat and crossed to the door, stooping down to look through the peephole. "Samantha?"

"Yes." She leaned to one side, revealing the wall of muscle behind her. "And Duke."

Should he feel guilty for being disappointed it wasn't Milo standing in the hall? Yeah. But he was too weary to bother, so he unlocked the door. "Why didn't you buzz?"

"I still have my key," Samantha replied sunnily, taking Duke's hand and leading him past Renner into the apartment.

"I assumed you wanted me to use it."

"That's a bit of a stretch," Renner said, closing the door and locking it. "But I'm not in the mood to argue."

"Oh no." Samantha blinked. "Are you sick?"

Did imaginary seasickness count? "No." Not wanting to court any form of sympathy, Renner courted irritation instead. "I don't have anything in the fridge but a flat bottle of Pellegrino and a wedge of Parmesan."

Duke looked like he was in pain. "Did no one teach you two the value of protein growing up?" He kissed Samantha's hand and lumbered back toward the door. "I have no choice. I have to stock the fridge. What's your favorite cut of meat?"

Renner started to protest Duke's mission to buy him groceries, especially because he was leaving for Manhattan and beyond soon, but he couldn't bring himself to deny the man his joy. Especially when Samantha tucked her hands beneath her chin and sighed dreamily.

"Surprise me," Renner muttered, earning a grunt from Duke.

When the door closed a second later, Renner turned to find Samantha leaning against the dining room table. "Duke knew I wanted to talk to you alone, but he needed to situate me first."

"Situate you. How romantic."

"Isn't it?" He barely recognized his sister with the heart-eyed canaries circling her head. "I didn't expect to get here and find you moping, though. Is something…wrong?"

Renner narrowed his eyes at his sister's hopeful tone. "Why do I get the feeling you already have something in mind?"

"Because you're so smart," Samantha responded, in a thick Boston accent. *Smaht.*

For the love of God. Renner breezed past his sister into the living room, picking up the remote and setting it back down without turning on the television. "Please tell me you didn't come here to ask me about Milo Bautista."

"Ding ding ding." She staggered toward him with her arms out. "I'm imagining myself handing you a giant game-show prize."

"I don't want it."

Samantha dropped her hands and frowned. "Come on, Renner. No one knows you like I do, so maybe they haven't noticed. But I've been watching *you* watch Milo for months. And then bowling happened." She dropped her voice to a whisper. "What else has happened?"

"Nothing." He untied his tie with jerky tugs. "Is this really why you came here?"

"Not the only reason." Samantha smoothed a hand over her stomach. "I'm pregnant and I'm here to ask you to be the godfather." Her bubbling laugh was pure joy. "I bet you feel pretty bad now for being snippy."

Renner was suddenly looking at Samantha through clouds. A flash of her as a gangly child rolled through his mind, then she was back, beaming at him in the living room. The tie was still in his hands but not off yet—that had to be the reason he was choking. "Jesus, Sam. Shit." He dropped the silk material and lunged forward, wrapping her in a hug. "That's...amazing. Even more amazing because you're not even...I mean, you don't seem nervous at all."

"No." She laid her head on his shoulder. "I can't believe it, either."

"Duke must be going crazy."

"He ripped the side off the house today so he could build an addition." She sniffed into his neck. "And I only told him this morning."

Renner pulled back, holding his sister by the arms. "Shit."

"I know! Shit!"

They smiled at each other, and several things occurred to

Renner at once. His sister had grown. Big-time. So much, she could function normally in a relationship. Something neither of them had thought possible once upon a time, because of her fear of abandonment. And he'd almost stolen that from her by trying to keep her and Duke apart. "Samantha, if you want someone else to be the godfather, I would understand."

Her smile disappeared. "I wouldn't have asked if I wanted someone else." She shoved him in the chest, but didn't budge him. "Duke wants you, too. It's a big, mushy circle of godfatherly want."

Christ. If he kept staring into his sister's big, happy eyes, he was going to embarrass himself, so he released her and stepped back. But the pressure continued to weigh down on his insides, forcing him to take a moment to speak. "I like Milo in a rather *objective* way."

"Try again, bro."

Yeah. She knew him too well. "He asked me to help him win another man."

"Oh, fuck."

"Samantha, watch your mouth around the baby."

Her hands fluttered. "See, I knew you'd be the best choice." She turned in a circle, as if looking for what to say. "Maybe there's an explanation. I'm not wrong about the way you guys…" She wiggled her fingers between them. "There's all *this* kind of thing going on."

"Living in New Jersey has made your hands very expressive. Use your words."

"Stop making me laugh," she wailed. "This is a crisis."

Renner's eyes strayed to the clock. If his night with Milo was still going to happen, he needed to be getting into the shower by now. But it wasn't happening, was it? Hell, maybe the guy had wised up and gone on his own.

That possibility was like a dagger being rammed through Renner's right eye.

"I wanted to help him, you know," Renner said, because stress was beginning to build below his neck and he needed to give it an outlet. Had he taken his pill today? It was hard to remember. Thinking of anything was growing more and more difficult, the later the evening grew. "I had to figure out everything on my own when I was young. I thought I could… give him a push. But I think maybe I was hoping he would just…"

"Want you instead?" Samantha tilted her head. "Maybe he does."

"I asked him." His eye sockets throbbed. "It didn't go well. You know how I handle things that don't go well. Or go *my way*, rather."

"Yes." Thankfully, there was no sympathy in her voice. He didn't want or deserve it. "Remember after the factory explosion, when you shook Duke's hand and apologized?"

"Nope, I forgot."

"You did *not*." Samantha softened. "Remember when you followed my husband into the factory, trying to stop him from getting exploded?"

Surprise prickled up Renner's spine. "He told you that?"

"Of course he did." Samantha reached out and squeezed his elbow. "There's another side to my brother. And if Milo asked you for help in the first place, he probably knows it's there." She tipped her head toward the door. "Go remind him."

Chapter Fourteen

Milo had just proven correct everyone who'd ever accused him of being an eternal optimist.

After the workday from hell, he'd dragged himself into the shower and put on the stupid starched-out jeans, which frankly made his balls feel like they were caught in an alligator's jaw. His hair was wet and finger-brushed, and he'd found a T-shirt similar to the red one he'd bought with Renner, yanking it over his head and fucking up his hair even more. And now he refused to fix it. Because that would have been the final proof that he actually thought his boss was showing up.

It wasn't happening. No one showed up for a night out with a guy who'd called him a prick. They'd been on uneven ground to begin with. Then the argument had illuminated every single difference between them. Every reason they shouldn't be friends…or more…to begin with. So as soon as eight o'clock arrived and Renner didn't appear at his door, Milo would suck it up and go remind him. He'd promised Renner he wasn't giving up on their friendship, and he'd damn well meant it.

The guy thought he could throw up a wall and Milo would bounce off? Well, he couldn't wait to see the guy's face when he kicked it down instead. Not for the first time, Milo's suspicion that Renner had been burned in the past was tingling. The defensiveness he'd seen the boss man display this afternoon was different from his typical sarcastic derision. If he played his cards right, maybe he could get to the bottom of what made Renner tick.

Milo was the first to admit his romantic life had been confusing—especially of late—but totally pain-free. It was easy for him to cast stones and call people pricks when he didn't know what a painful breakup felt like. Did Renner know?

Why did he suddenly want to smash things with his fists?

Milo's gaze cut toward the clock. Seven fifty-nine. The damn thing had crawled toward their original meeting time, then sped up, hadn't it? *Not coming. He's not coming.*

Refusing to listen for the sound of footsteps coming up the stairs, Milo went to the bedroom and jerked the hated leather jacket off its hanger, shoving his arms into it. Inside his head, he began rehearsing the speech he would give Renner, soon as the guy opened his apartment door. *Surprise, motherfucker.* No, that wouldn't fly. How about, *Do these jeans make my ass look big? Tell me on the way to the city.*

Lame.

Milo grabbed his keys and cell phone on the way toward the door. Before he could throw it open, however, he heard a creak on the other side.

He froze.

"I can see your feet beneath the door," Renner called, and Milo mouthed a curse. "Actually, I've been out here listening to you abuse hangers and call the clock a bitch."

How could he want to strangle this man one minute and make out with him the next? "That must have been coming from across the hall."

"I'll pretend that's true if you open the door."

Milo needed a minute to dim the smile on his face. Opening the door like a high school kid waiting for his prom date would be equivalent to forgiving Renner for being a prick. And while he kind of thought Renner showing up in the first place was the boss's way of apologizing, Milo wasn't quite ready to call it even. Pressing his lips together, Milo opened the door and leaned against the jamb, arms crossed. Trying to be aloof. Which was a lot harder than he'd anticipated, because Renner looked…fucking phenomenal. "Well. The door is open."

"I see that." Renner gave him a once-over that reminded Milo he'd forgotten to clear the pipes while getting ready, because yeah, that was his dick stiffening into a crowbar. "I also see you were getting ready to go without me."

Lie to him, the devil on his shoulder whispered. He wouldn't even have to confirm or deny. Just shrug or stay silent. If Renner had encountered a mirror in his crisp, fitted white button-down shirt and charcoal-gray slacks, his ego could probably use a dent or two. *Damn*, he was gorgeous. But letting Renner believe something that wasn't true didn't sit right with Milo. Nor did it accomplish his goal of getting Renner to open up. "No, actually. I was on my way to you." Satisfaction warmed Milo when Renner couldn't hide his relief, the lines around his eyes softening, his huge shoulders deflating. "I was worried I'd get there and you'd already be halfway to Manhattan. For good."

"I thought about it," Renner murmured, watching Milo from beneath heavy eyelids. "But I made a deal with someone, and I haven't met my side of it yet."

Gravity was trying to suck Milo into the hallway toward Renner, but he withstood the magnetic draw. "I haven't met mine, either."

"Yes, you have." Renner ran a finger along the inside of his collar, sending a woodsy, expensive scent in Milo's direction, making his belt feel ever tighter. "So. You were right today. I was a prick." It wasn't easy for his boss to say those words, which made them twice as meaningful. "I should have…"

"What?"

Renner gave him an exasperated look. "Perhaps a hug was required." His visible irritation was belied by his unnatural tone, his throat muscles shifting. "I should have told you, before any of it started, that your idea about pitching the competitors was brilliant. I'm…at ease. Because of that idea. Because of what you said…about me. So your end of the deal is complete." One corner of his mouth jumped. "If I'd known you were so bloodthirsty, I would have hired you to work upstairs."

"I'm happy where I am," Milo managed around the papier-mâché lining his throat. "And I'm only bloodthirsty when someone screws with one of my friends."

His boss was still a moment before putting his hand out for a shake. "Friends."

Everything about the situation was right. And wrong. At the same time. How was that possible? Where exactly had the wrong turns been taken? Half of Milo was relieved his friendship with Renner was intact, and the other half? Not so much. Shaking hands felt…symbolic. Like this afternoon would be the last time Renner looked down at him and asked, *You loved it in general? Or just with me?* His feelings about Renner weren't in focus yet, but Milo knew he wanted Renner to ask him those questions again. Soon.

Just not yet. Which meant he had no choice but to shake, right?

Swallowing hard, Milo took Renner's hand and squeezed. "Friends."

• • •

As predicted, they hit traffic on the way into Manhattan, but Renner was more than happy to put off walking into Phoenix—the club—with Milo. As soon as they walked through the doors, their time together would be divided into before and after. Right now, Renner was the only man who'd touched Milo. The only man who'd spoken to him as more than a buddy. Ten minutes from now, it wouldn't be that way. There would be interest thrown in Milo's direction. Probably a shit-ton of it, too, because people were going to respond to the energy given off by the glass-half-full security guard from Boston.

Renner wasn't a fanciful man who believed in auras or any kind of voodoo bullshit, but there was no denying Milo had an air that wasn't typical to anyone, let alone a club full of New Yorkers who would cut through a phony facade like warm butter. And Milo didn't have one. He represented on the surface everything lying beneath. Two blocks from the club, walking on foot from the parking garage where Renner had left the car, men and women were already taking notice of him.

Probably because he couldn't stop fidgeting with the stupid jacket.

"I hate this jacket."

Renner had this impulse. It was insane, but he actually had to talk himself out of throwing Milo over one shoulder and heaving him into a cab. His apartment in Gramercy was only a short ride from the East Village. "Yes, I know you hate the jacket. That much is obvious." He stuffed his hand into his pocket to keep from holding Milo's hand. "Why did you wear it?"

He could sense Milo smiling. "You want the truth?"

"Always."

"Well, I was hoping if I showed up at your apartment wearing it, you would laugh. And then our argument would be halfway to over." Seriously. This time of night, they could be at Renner's place in no time. "When you showed up, I forgot to take it off and now I'm stuck with it. So there you go."

Up ahead, Phoenix came into view, and Renner's gut rebelled. "Is your accent getting thicker?"

"Yeah." They stopped at the corner to wait for traffic to pass, Milo scrubbing at the back of his neck. "It happens when I'm anxious."

"Don't worry," Renner said, striving for casual. "It's going to work in your favor."

"Huh." Milo eyed him. "So what's going to happen when we get inside? I probably should have asked on the way over, but I liked that music you were playing."

"Really."

"Yeah, really." Milo gave him an elbow in the ribs. "What was it? Sounded old."

Renner should have felt like a high school student, talking about his musical taste, but he didn't. He...*wanted* to share something with Milo. Probably because he was getting ready to walk into a club and share Milo with everyone else. The crossing signal turned green, and a pounding started in his temples. "Robert Johnson, and yes, it's very old." He took Milo's elbow and guided him past a crowd of loud twentysomethings blocking the sidewalk. "There's a legend that says Johnson sold his soul to the devil and asked to become the best blues player in the world."

"I never pegged you for a blues guy." He could sense Milo watching him as they walked. "So how did selling his soul pan out?"

"It worked. We're still talking about him eighty years later, right?" They were almost to the door, and Renner's need to keep walking, right past the entrance, was severe. "He died when he was twenty-seven, but at least he left a legacy behind."

Milo pulled him to a stop, paying zero attention to the bouncer who held out a hand for identification. Not Renner's ID. Only Milo's. *Fucker.* "Selling your soul to be the best," he said, his fingers digging into Renner's elbow. "Working yourself into an early grave. I don't like the way you say that like it makes sense. Or like you can relate."

"You're making something out of nothing."

"Am I?" Milo whipped out his wallet and slipped the doorman his ID without breaking eye contact with Renner. "Are you living or just trying to stay alive?"

Something pointed stuck itself just above Renner's collarbone and wouldn't budge. Was he resentful of the question? Yes. Because it struck the mark. He'd been buried in work and routine and numbers so long, he couldn't remember what life had been like before. This wasn't news, though. He'd been aware for a while now that he was working himself to death. But there'd never been a reason to stop. No light at the end of the tunnel.

The man in front of him couldn't be that light. No.

Yes, he was a son of a bitch, but he wouldn't be selfish with Milo. Where they stood at that very moment was symbolic. Renner would rather saw off his own arm than drag him back from the precipice of a new beginning.

"You asked what would happen when we got inside," Renner said, changing the subject. He ushered Milo into a lit hallway leading to the main floor of the club, giving the doorman a sour look as they passed. "I hope it's not too late to inform you, but…they make newcomers do the funky chicken on stage. Naked."

Milo laughed. "Shut up."

Renner pulled back a velvet curtain, swallowing nails as Milo passed through. "We're going to do the same thing one does at any bar. We're going to get a drink."

"Okay. I know drinking."

It was kind of hysterical watching Milo strut into the noisy club. His thousand-yard stare paired with his loose-hipped swagger reminded Renner of the way men entered the Third Shift. Like they were sizing the place up as a potential location for scratching their nuts and watching baseball for the night. The sandwich Renner had eaten that afternoon turned to a stone in his stomach as heads started to turn, the customers more than a little curious about the newcomer. If Renner had to guess, they were probably wondering one of two things. If Renner and Milo were together. Or if Renner had dragged a straight guy in off the street.

Was it wrong that Renner would be relieved if they landed on either conclusion?

Yes. Definitely.

"Try to be a little less intimidating," Renner called over the music, finding them a sliver of room at the packed bar. "Right now, you are basically a *Law & Order* cop walking into a club to question the bartender about a murder."

"I doubt the jacket from hell is helping." Milo shook off the faux leather bomber and shoved it beneath one tattoo-covered arm. "Better?"

Bettah?

"Yeah." Renner cleared the sudden hunger from his throat, because *good God.* Leaning against the bar with his chin up and ankles crossed, biceps on display, Milo was... hot as fuck. No way around it. Blue ink decorated his arms straight down to either wrist, stubble darkening his jaw. A sharp, thoughtful, eager man, wrapped in a bad-boy fantasy outer shell. The fact that the music hadn't skipped and halted when they walked into the bar was beyond Renner.

"You want to dance?" Milo asked, both dimples making an appearance.

"I think you know the answer to that."

A shrug that Renner could see held some disappointment. "Worth a shot."

Behind Milo, a man was visibly interested, sipping his drink as he tried to decipher the dynamic between Renner and Milo. Grinding his jaw together, Renner caught one of the bartenders' attention and ordered Milo a beer, plus a whiskey for himself. "I think it might be a good idea if we separate," Renner managed, even with the snake coiling around his neck. "Just for a while. I don't want to keep anyone from talking to you."

And I sure as hell don't want a front-row seat.

Chapter Fifteen

Milo's first swig of beer hit his stomach like a bomb.

He didn't want Renner to go away. Not even a little bit.

Was it nerves? Because those things were riding unicycles on his pancreas. Phoenix was like the Land of Oz compared to the dive bars Milo frequented on nights out. Not only because men were dancing with men — and the bartenders were wearing vests with no shirt underneath — but the atmosphere was intimidating in itself. Everyone was so comfortable, talking and laughing like they had lifetime memberships at the club. The music was so loud he could feel the bass pumping in his groin, which wasn't an altogether unpleasant feeling, but along with watching men acting so unrestrained together…he could admit to feeling aroused. Just from the sudden freedom to watch. To be interested, if he so chose.

All this time, places like Phoenix had existed around him and he'd never considered going. Now that he was inside, all the impulses he'd been dealing with alone didn't feel so huge or unmanageable.

So apart from the typical fear of looking like a rookie on

the first day of practice, he wasn't necessarily nervous. No, the squeeze and release in his belly had to do with Renner.

Currently, his boss was scoping the bar, looking for a convenient place to keep an eye on Milo. But not be *too* near. Because that would be bad, right? Yeah. Milo definitely didn't want Renner to tug him closer by the waistband of his jeans and warn everyone off. Right.

Or had it taken this moment of separation to realize Renner's claiming him in front of everyone was *exactly* what he wanted?

Logically, Milo knew this experience was healthy for him. Hadn't he asked Renner to help him talk to men? Not about sports or cars, but in an interested kind of way? Yes, he had. The way he hadn't been capable of speaking to Travis. Now that the moment had arrived, he couldn't be sure if he wanted Renner—instead of anyone else in the room or possibly the planet—because Renner was all he *knew*.

Although, as Renner paid for the drinks and began to sidle away…the contractions in Milo's stomach shifted higher. *Higher*. Until his heart was center of attention. The beer in Milo's hand sweated down his knuckles and he could feel every trickle, could feel answering perspiration run down his spine. Renner was giving him an encouraging nod that didn't come anywhere near his eyes. So what did that mean? Was he waiting for Milo to decide if he stayed or went?

"Relax, Bautista." He was back to Bautista, was he? "I'm not going far. I'll be right over there if you need me."

I need you.

It was that sharp jab of thought that prevented Milo from stopping Renner. He *couldn't* already need him. That had to be the nervous energy talking. Or the fact that he'd only ever touched one man. Only ever given and received pleasure from one man. There was a gravitational pull toward Renner, but he couldn't allow it to take him. Not until he was positive what was causing it. Lust, familiarity, or…something more.

The *something more* pulled into first place when Renner's back was swallowed up by the crowd. Milo's gaze followed his boss's progress until he reappeared in full on the other side of the bar. They frowned at each other across the distance and stupidly, Milo would have been content to proceed to scowl at Renner all night. But Renner tilted his head and gave him a look that said *knock it off and have fun.*

Right. Fun.

Fun wasn't easy when you were tied in a dozen knots, trying to stay grounded in reality, instead of rounding the bar and giving Renner hell for…what? Getting under his skin?

"Excuse me." Milo turned when the man beside him spoke. "I hope I'm not intruding, but I wanted to make sure that wasn't your boyfriend before I bought you a drink."

"I…uh." Milo glanced down at the bottle in his hand, shocked to find it empty. Then he looked at Renner, who appeared to be engrossed by his phone—asshole—before turning back to the man on his left. The stranger reminded him a little of Travis. Blond. Easy smile. But he didn't feel the tug of attraction he'd experienced with Travis. Or the avalanche he'd gotten buried under with Renner. "No, he's not my boyfriend."

"Great." The guy nodded, appearing pretty relieved, which put Milo at ease. As much as it were possible while torn in half. "I'm Chris."

"Milo."

"Milo." Chris inched closer so they could hear each other over the music…and every hair on Milo's neck stood up. In that way that happens when something is off. Wrong. "Where are you from? Do I hear Boston?"

Talking to a dude while being given not-so-subtle once-overs was new. *Very* new. Milo even forced himself to do the same. And found out pretty quickly that he was a critical jerkwad. While he did find Chris attractive, his shoulders weren't wide enough. His voice wasn't deep enough. He didn't give Milo any bullshit or try to argue, so the conversation was a little more flirtatious than he was comfortable with. And the entire time, his focus went into not seeking out Renner's gaze across the bar. Which was a feat of epic proportions, considering he could feel the burn of a certain factory owner on him all the while. *Do something about it, Renner.*

Another man approached and Chris introduced him. After a few minutes of talking, the newcomer started to laugh. "I keep waiting for you to realize you're in the wrong place."

"Who, me?" Milo tugged on his collar. "Why's that?"

The two men exchanged an amused look. "No reason, I guess. You just don't strike me as the club type," Chris said. "That's not a good or bad thing. Just an observation."

"We were going to dance," the new guy said, tipping his head toward the mass of bodies toward the back of the space. "Want to join?"

Milo loved to dance. He would probably shock these two city boys into making a whole *new* observation about him, because God knew, he could move like nobody's business. But it took until that moment, with two men trying to edge him toward the dance floor, to realize why there was a yawning pit in the center of his stomach. He was still waiting for Renner to come get him. Those stolen moments in the hammock, the dressing room, out in the bowling alley parking lot, and the factory office…they were all cycling past in perfect clarity.

I make the decisions. Boss inside work. Boss outside of work. That's me.

Milo had to shift the way he stood because his dick grew thick with the memories. Yeah. Where was the man who made the rules? He wanted that man. Now. Whether or not it was realistic, or even smart at this point in time, he'd spent the entire conversation wanting Renner to wrap a hand around the back of his neck. *He's taken.* What would it be like to hear those words from Renner...and know they pertained to him?

This was ridiculous. He wanted *one* man. What was he doing with two others?

Worrying about how much whiskey Renner was drinking and if alcohol consumption allowed his heart pills to function. That's what he was doing. And remembering that story about Robert Johnson dying at twenty-seven after selling his soul to the devil. His boss was a probable millionaire and only in his early thirties, but how much longer could he pull seven-day workweeks off? Who was going to look after him when he left Hook?

Shit. He was leaving. Maybe he wouldn't even bother traveling back with Milo, since they were already in Manhattan.

Milo wasn't the type to play games with anyone, but he couldn't deny the sudden anger flickering in his chest. Over being touched with such possessiveness, only to be set loose with so little thought. Left to his own devices in a club full of men. Left in Hook. Alcohol fizzed and popped in his veins, making those sweaty memories between him and Renner just a little too vivid. A little too real. The guy was just going to sit there and watch him flirt with two men? Renner had been in his mouth a matter of hours ago, holding Milo's hair like he owned him. Didn't that mean something?

You always knew he was out of your league.

He probably can't wait to off-load you onto someone else.

"Yeah." Milo drained his fourth beer and plonked the empty bottle down onto the bar, refusing to glance in Renner's direction. Mostly because he was afraid the prick would still be staring at his phone, not caring one way or the other how Milo spent his night. "Let's go dance."

Getting a prompt *holy shit* out of Chris and his friend was pretty gratifying, Milo had to admit. Didn't matter that he'd never danced with a man—dancing was dancing. And he'd been turning his mother around the kitchen since childhood, before moving on to the girls at his Boston middle school. They'd fought over a turn with him at dances, because they'd known he would make them look good and not try to play grab-ass, like a lot of boys his age.

"You're full of surprises," Chris said behind him, moving closer. Close enough that Milo could feel the other guy's breath on his neck, the hand coasting over his hip. The third member of their party moved in from the other side, sandwiching Milo, a secret smile on his face. It was so easy, so smooth. On the outside, at least. Inside Milo, hell was breaking loose. He closed his eyes and tried to calm the clamoring alarm in his bloodstream. Cheating. It felt like cheating, no matter which angle he looked at it from. Had he really gone out to the dance floor hoping to force Renner into reacting? How *was* he reacting?

Milo tried to picture Renner rolling his hips in between two men—and his stomach heaved so violently, he had to extricate himself from the other men, every hair on his body standing straight up. "I'm sorry. I—" He waved a hand between them. "You guys go ahead."

Chris looked as though he understood. "We'll be here if you change your mind."

Needing to get to Renner, Milo turned on a heel and began weaving through the crowd, which had grown a ton since they'd arrived. A speech wrote itself inside his head as he tried to spot a pair of hockey shoulders at the bar. *Stop acting like you don't care about us, boss man. You broke your rules for me. I know you feel something. I do, too. A huge, complicated something. Let's go back to Jersey and figure it the fuck out.*

But when the crowd parted and he saw a man touching Renner, the speech cut off like a loudspeaker being dropped into the ocean. The man was trying to tug Renner away from the bar, presumably to the same dance floor Milo had just vacated. He was dressed much the same as Renner in expensive clothing, his demeanor that of a man who ran business meetings and had an expense account. Renner was laughing as the man urged him to join everyone on the floor, but the corners of the boss man's eyes weren't crinkled, which meant the laugh wasn't authentic.

And yet, Milo authentically didn't give a rat's ass.

He'd swallowed a hammer. Or an anvil. Or something bulky and misshapen. But he was on the move anyway, sliding through conversations without so much as an apology, his blood buzzing like a beehive. No one touched Renner. No one.

No one.

Renner's own sister, Samantha, had tried to clock Renner outside the factory once, and Milo had been incapable of even letting *that* happen, comeuppance be damned.

Jealousy sent fireworks going off over Milo's head, but there was shame laced in. For damn sure. Because despite how he'd tried to justify dancing with Chris to himself, he'd been trying to make Renner jealous. Now he was getting a taste of his own medicine…and he'd been dosed with poison instead. He'd only ever been mildly jealous over Travis dating so many men. This was nothing like that. Milo's neck was so hot, he marveled that it hadn't burst into flames yet. Had he really wondered if his feelings for Renner were a product of proximity?

He'd been a giant idiot.

Finally, Milo reached Renner and Fuck Face. It appeared Renner had just given in and agreed to dance, which set Milo off even more. He stepped in between his boss and the too-aggressive man and shoved. "Step. Off. He said no." His breath raked in over a bed of thorns. "You can't just—just *handle* people like that."

"Whoa." The guy recovered from his stumble, approaching again with palms out. "Actually, he said yes, but I don't want any problems."

Milo flexed his fingers. "Looks like you found one anyway, didn't you, pal?"

"*Milo*," Renner said behind him, voice sharp. "That's enough. You're being ridiculous."

"Am I?" According to everyone gaping at him, yes. Yes, he was. But his chest wasn't done flooding with panic and relief and jealousy. The realization he'd come to on the dance floor, which was, he'd probably die if he saw Renner with someone else. And then it had *happened*. "He…" Milo jabbed a finger at Fuck Face. "He probably shouldn't even be dancing, okay? He has a *heart* condition."

"Oh for the love of *God*," Renner groaned behind him. "Just kill me now. End it."

Fuck Face actually began to look pretty sympathetic, which was Milo's first clue he didn't only *feel* lost, he looked it, too. The man who'd dared touch Renner patted Milo on the shoulder and leaned down to whisper in his ear. "Not that he isn't gorgeous as shit, but I asked him to dance because he looked completely miserable. I'm guessing you have something to do with that." He straightened. "Have fun fixing it."

Chapter Sixteen

Renner was ready to launch into this century's greatest reproof. They were literally going to pen odes in tribute. Milo didn't even *know* what was coming his way.

After spending a gut-wrenching five minutes watching Milo being fawned over—*touched*—the dick thought he could storm over and prevent Renner from doing the same? Never mind that Renner was about as inclined to dance as he was to shotgun a gallon of lighter fluid, but that wasn't the point. Hell *no*, it wasn't.

The point was—

Milo turned around, and Renner's reproof leaked out through his ears.

The sarcastic, quick-witted charmer from Boston looked like he'd just been informed his puppy had died. Oh, there was still some residual irritation etched into his features, too, but it was being tossed about in a sea of *well fuck, everything hurts, doesn't it?*

Renner was terrified of the hope that bloomed in his midsection. Terrified to think of what lay behind Milo's torn-up expression. So he tried to wrangle his earlier wrath, but it came out sounding half assed. "That was unacceptable. Out of line doesn't even begin to cover it."

"I know."

"You know." Renner's hands kept opening and closing, wanting to reach for Milo, so he fisted them and forced them to remain at his side. "Here we are again. That place where I'm left wondering where you get off thinking you have the right to stand between me and...anything. Be it bodily harm, being mugged, or dancing."

"Maybe I don't have the right," Milo said, so low Renner needed to strain to make out his words over the music. "Especially not after I tried to make you jealous."

"That's—what?"

Milo stepped into Renner's space, their thighs brushing, his mouth coming so close Renner wet his lips without thinking. "You heard me."

Yes, he'd heard him. Loud and clear. And Renner didn't know what reaction Milo desired after that pronouncement, but it probably wasn't the jealousy that came rushing back in full force. Maybe even stronger than he'd felt it while watching other men touch...*his* man. Renner's teeth snapped together of their own accord, his forehead grinding against Milo's. "You don't think *I* wanted go over there and start a fight of my own?"

"Did you?" Milo's exhale bathed his lips. "I've seen that right hook. It's nasty."

Don't. Don't feel an explosion of male pride over that—
Too late.

"Yeah?" They were both breathing hard. "I wanted to give *you* one a minute ago."

Milo pressed their laps together and both men reached at the same time, dragging each other closer by the hips. Forcibly. "What changed?"

There was no lying when they were pressed together head to toe, words being delivered right into each other's mouths. "You looked upset," Renner rasped.

"I *was* fucking upset. I've been upset since you walked away and left me standing there." Milo tilted his chin up and their lips locked together, but they didn't kiss. "I'm upset right now, too, but I don't really know why. Why, Renner?"

Because the whole situation was a certified mess. Their attraction to each other was off the goddamn map. Despite their insane differences, they...*worked*. Which was incredible, but true. Renner had never been an overly romantic person, finding flattery and closeness difficult to bear, because his youth had been more about independence. This, right here... this closeness with Milo wasn't forced or uncomfortable at all. It was like he'd found a lit-up harbor and could finally drop his anchor. But their course together had started out with Milo wanting to land another man. And Renner's insecurities were so wrapped up in that fact, he couldn't let it go. He'd managed to ignore the ground trembling at first, but now that Milo in his life could be a reality, doubts were popping up like weeds in an otherwise beautiful garden.

"I asked you a question, boss man."

Being called the boss made Renner growl low in his throat. "You're upset because..." *Because you can sense I'm not 100 percent in.* "You're upset because you were forced to abandon your dance to come defend my honor."

Milo's eyes narrowed as if he wanted to argue, but the mood had shifted away from anger. And it had shifted *hard*. At some point, they'd begun to sway to the music, and Milo's cock was sliding side to side against Renner's abdomen, fat and needy. Renner's dick was wedged to the side, but with a discreet glance at their surroundings, he reached into his dress pants and adjusted it so they could rub their erections together. *Sweet fuck*, watching Milo's eyes roll back in his head was better than landing any account. Hell, it was the beginning of an *obsession*.

"No, I…" Milo visibly struggled to retain the thoughts in his head, all while they bumped and ground. "I didn't stop dancing to come get Fuck Face off of you. I'd already stopped. I was going to…"

Renner barely managed to contain a snort over "Fuck Face." "You were going to what?"

Milo moaned, his stomach hollowing. "I was going to ask what happened to the boss. Inside work. Outside work. That's what you told me, but I didn't think *that* man would let me out of his sight." His eyes challenged Renner. "Guess I was wrong."

Oh. Oh hell no. He sure as hell hadn't expected Milo to say that, which probably accounted for the speeding train of denial that rammed right into his stomach. The muscles in his neck and back grew uncomfortably tight, like they might snap. It was a fucking wake-up call. There was no other way to describe it. Milo was right. What the fuck had he been thinking bringing Milo here and letting other hands touch him? He must have placed some kind of mental block on the reality of how wrong it was. Now, that dam had cracked straight down the center, and the possessiveness he felt when touching Milo came pouring in. "I wouldn't have let you leave with anyone," Renner rasped. "God no. I wouldn't have been able to handle that."

"Why?" Milo prodded. "Tell me, Renner, because I needed you to…mark me. I kept waiting and you never came. So I need to hear the reason you wouldn't let me leave with anyone."

Renner wasn't used to being questioned, and with anyone else, he would have shut it down by now. It wasn't even that he owed it to Milo to answer…no. He *wanted* to. It felt natural. Everything about having this man's body firm and full of life against his provoked honesty. He could say anything. Things that sounded stupid or smart. Because Milo would either understand or give him shit for it. And wasn't that a fantastic fucking certainty? "Because I want you for myself."

Milo exhaled in a rush. "Okay. *Good*, dammit. I want you, too." The club lights flashed in his eyes. Blue, pink, red. "You said it. I said it. No going back now." He paused. "I need the boss man. All the time. That part of you can't take any more vacations."

Renner closed his eyes, and for the first time in forever, let something other than his mind do the talking. Because Milo needed it. "I want to take you home and…do things to you. Things that make you moan into my sheets. And yeah, Milo, I want to be the boss during all of it." Milo's racing breath told him to keep going. "Next time you come to my office on a lunch break, I want you to sit on my desk and get sucked off. You're going to be that employee that gets extra-special treatment from the boss, and I don't give a fuck who complains about it. For everyone that's got something to say, I'll put my tongue in your mouth on the factory floor."

Milo's hands twisted in the waistband of Renner's pants. "I think you b-better stop talking or I'm not going to be able to walk out of here upright."

"I'm not done."

"Can you tell me the rest later? When we're somewhere I can jack off?" Milo turned their bodies and pushed forward, beginning to openly hump Renner against the bar. He kept them under the guise of dancing by staying in sync with the fast, pounding music, but anyone with a brain knew they were two zippers away from fucking in public. A filthy, frantic point that Renner had never reached in private, let alone in a packed club. "I'm so hot right now. I can't hear anymore."

"That's too bad." Renner scraped his teeth down Milo's neck. "You're going to take my cock tonight, pretty boy. I'm going to watch those tattoos flex and sweat while you take your first man and afterward...afterward, I think, I'm going to kiss you." Okay. *This* was a detour. "I'm going to kiss your mouth and ask you questions I already know the answer to. Just because I like the way you say certain words with that accent." The corner of Milo's lips edged up and a laugh puffed out. "I'm going to make sure you're okay about how I took you. How it felt. If it was too hard or fast. And I'll know whether or not you're lying by your eyes."

"You won't catch me lying, boss man."

"Lyin'," Renner repeated. "See, I knew you would say it that way."

Milo's gaze dropped to his mouth, and he just kind of stared, his hips giving a slow roll that had Renner biting back a curse. "Is this really happening?"

A memory of Milo on the dance floor between two men surfaced, along with the way he'd spoken about Travis initially. How his eyes had sparkled with humor while describing the chef. Renner pushed those memories to one side and focused on different thoughts. The way Milo had looked charging through the crowd to get between him and...Fuck Face. Or how he looked now, eyelids heavy with lust and hope tingeing his voice. All these different doubts and possibilities rumbled in the wrestling ring of Renner's mind and in the end, neither of them claimed victory.

Necessity won the battle, instead. He needed Milo tonight. Milo needed him.

Tomorrow, Renner would fight the next war.

The one with his mind.

Chapter Seventeen

Milo tried to play it cool as he walked into Renner's apartment. Then he caught a glimpse of his face in the entry hall mirror and was forced to accept he wasn't pulling it off. Not by a damn sight. His sudden case of clammy hands probably had something to do with Renner's doorman being dressed better than him. Or the hallway—hell, the elevator—having nicer carpet than his apartment back in Hook.

All those dents in his self-confidence came *before* he actually turned the corner and viewed the living room.

He hadn't been intimidated by his boss's apartment back in Hook, because the unfurnished, no-nonsense space hadn't spoken of Renner's wealth. Well, this place was going to lose its fucking voice, it was screaming so loud. Tasteful, masculine. Polished, pricey. All of those descriptions fit the gigantic space with a view overlooking downtown Manhattan. Renner didn't even have to bother turning on a light, because the glittering city illuminated the dark living space for them. White light bounced off chrome finishing on the oversize coffee table, the stocked wine cabinet, and gleaming wooden mantelpiece.

Navy-blue runners ran behind the modern-style couch, then off toward the kitchen, which lay in the opposite direction. God, it even smelled like crispy money that had been spritzed with Hugo Boss. Or whatever the expensive version of Hugo Boss happened to be.

Behind Milo, Renner cleared his throat. "Are you hungry? The fridge should be stocked."

Who did that? Fairies? "I can always eat." *Get out of your head and stop questioning your right to be here.* Fastening a smile onto his face, Milo turned and leaned against the breakfast bar that looked into the kitchen. "You have any cereal?"

"Cereal." Renner paused in the act of retrieving two liquor tumblers from the cabinet. "It's nearly midnight and you want cereal?"

"If we're talking about things we want, I wish we were back in the club." Until the words came out of his mouth, Milo hadn't even been aware of their existence. "You got weird on me during the ride over. And now I'm getting weird on you because this place is like a fucking palace." Milo shook his head and laughed a little. "I just want us back kissing in that club."

Renner's hand was suspended in midair, holding a bottle of Johnnie Walker. "I don't know if you saying that made it less weird. Or weirder."

"Me, either." Milo hopped up onto one of the breakfast stools, sighing over how comfortable the damn thing was. Like a cloud for his ass. "But I usually figure things out over a bowl of Frosted Mini-Wheats. Do you have anything resembling that? Or does everything in your apartment contain quinoa?"

"Hey, you're the one on *my* case about being healthier."

"Cereal doesn't count." Milo grinned. "Everyone knows that."

Renner gave him a skeptical face, then poured two

generous portions of whiskey into each glass, sliding one in Milo's direction. "I have Grape Nuts."

Milo dropped his head into his hands. "Fuck my life."

When he looked up again, Renner was placing a bowl and spoon in front of him...and an unopened box of Peanut Butter Crunch. "Gotcha."

Oh man. Wow. The way Renner winked at Milo sucked the breath out of his lungs. Or maybe it was how he stood, hip propped against the counter in his socks, nursing whiskey. So cool and in charge, that arrogant head tilt out to play. Or maybe he wasn't so in control, because what he said next made Milo spill cereal on the counter mid-pour.

"I got weird on you because I don't usually bring men to my home." Renner's mouth hovered just above the edge of his glass. "There's usually a designated meeting place. Somewhere neutral and impersonal. It's all very clear-cut."

Milo poured the milk. "And this...isn't."

Renner raised an eyebrow. "Do you think it is?"

"No." He took his time chewing the first bite of cereal. "I got weird on you because this place is a lot nicer than I expected." He set down the spoon. "Actually, I couldn't even have expected this level of nice in a million years because I've never seen anything like it. Who stocks your fridge?"

"The concierge."

"Well...okay. Sure." Ignoring the roiling in his stomach, Milo hopped off the stool. "So it's all out on the table, right? You're weird because you have boundary issues and I'm weird because I couldn't afford your ottoman. Is that it?"

Renner inclined his head and looked away. A yes? It felt like a no. Until Renner took a swallow of his drink and said, "There is something else."

The bottom of Milo's stomach dropped out and hit the floor. Oh Jesus. It could be anything, couldn't it? Maybe he was a DC Comics fanatic and needed to warn Milo before they went into his Batman-themed bedroom. "Yeah?"

The boss man stared at Milo so long, he wondered if the guy had fallen into a trance. "Um." Renner finished his drink in one swallow. "Samantha and Duke are having a baby. They've asked me to be the godfather."

"What?" Milo did a double take. "Not a Batman room."

Renner reared back. "What was that?"

"Never mind." Milo put his hands on his hips and laughed. "Holy shit—that's amazing. Duke must be losing his mind."

"That's what I said."

"In a good way."

"Yes."

There was a melting sensation in Milo's stomach, put there by the way Renner ducked his head, as if he didn't want another human being to see him smile. "You're nervous about being the godfather. I can tell. But you're going to be the badass that gets to swoop in with presents and fly away. Like Batman. That's what I meant...when I said that..."

"Is it?" Renner's eyes narrowed as he poured himself a second glass of Johnnie Walker. "Because—"

Thankful for a distraction, Milo grabbed Renner's wrist. "Whiskey and heart pills don't make good bunkmates." When Renner rolled his eyes, Milo brushed his thumb across the inside of Renner's wrist and felt his pulse kick. "For me?"

After a short stare-down, Renner set the bottle on the counter. "You seem pretty sure I would make concessions for you."

Ah God. The boss man's voice had deepened. A lot. It smoked out from between Renner's lips and slithered in between Milo's ribs, gathering in his stomach, like a living thing. "Yeah...maybe I am sure you'll make concessions for me. But I don't know why."

Renner advanced, backing Milo across the kitchen, stopping a breath away from where Milo's hips met the opposite counter. "I don't know either, because I've never had to think about it before." He ran his tongue along his bottom lip, then reached down and began unfastening Milo's jeans. "But if I had to guess, I would say...I want to make you happy. In this kitchen. Everywhere." His knuckles pushed down on Milo's erection while their gazes held. "And I want to give you victories, so you'll let me take mine in bed. Does that make sense?"

"Yes." Milo probably would have said anything as long as Renner didn't stop finding the fastest way to his cock. His erection had been stretching out his underwear since they'd driven into Manhattan together hours earlier, and it just wanted to be *used*. It remembered that hand job in the dressing room and was aching for more. Truthfully, though, Renner's explanation did make sense. The man in front of him liked to dominate, liked to call the shots, and since Milo had a lot of pride, he countered that aggression by giving in elsewhere. Somehow it worked, and Milo didn't want to question a damn thing. Not now, when he was so turned on he could barely see straight. "I-it makes sense."

Renner shoved a hand into the opening he'd created in Milo's jeans, taking hold of his dick and almost making his knees lose power. "Those concessions no longer include dancing with other men. I want to be goddamn clear about that."

Milo literally could not control the sound that escaped him. It might have been the first whimper of his life, but ask him if he was ashamed. The answer was no. Was it unbelievable that he felt like he'd slipped into a second skin? Yes. But there it was. Nodding at Renner's demand while the man held him in a don't-fuck-with-me grip was exactly where he wanted to be. Nowhere else. Not to mention, his heart was pounding in an erratic Morse code of its own over Renner's taking verbal ownership. The specific kind. The kind he'd been craving tonight back at the club, and now that he had it, exhilaration blew up his spine. "You've made yourself clear," Milo managed around the tightness in his throat. "That's exactly what I need, too."

"Good." Renner stroked him. Hard. So hard Milo's legs kicked back and pounded against the kitchen counter. "Get this cock into my bed where it belongs."

When he released Milo, they squared off a little. Like two boxers who'd gone one round and learned each other's flavor, but there hadn't been a knockout yet. There was a promise floating between them that said it was coming, though. Maybe more than once and in different forms. But Milo had never been a coward, so he stripped off his shirt and tossed it over his shoulder, watching Renner's eyes darken as he strutted toward the bedroom.

And damn *right* he followed.

Milo caught a glimpse in the panoramic window of Renner unbuttoning his shirt and coming after him. Despite his bravado and catwalk stroll, a rave was taking place in his stomach. For several reasons. What if he disappointed Renner with his inexperience? What if he was rushing into something he wasn't ready for? Hell, what did he know about sex with a man, apart from being incredibly aware that the idea got him hot like crazy?

Relax.

"Relax," Renner breathed into his neck, gliding a hand down Milo's abdomen. His fingertips stopped just short of Milo's cock, brushing back and forth across his happy trail. "I'm an aggressive man, and I won't hold back about what I want to do with you in bed." He laid a hard kiss beneath Milo's right ear. "But if you're uncomfortable at any time, we'll stop and go eat Cap'n Crunch."

The tension eased from Milo's muscles. "I'm even more sure I want this after hearing you say that." He turned to find

Renner without a shirt and— "Jesus Christ, boss man."

"What?"

"You're built like a brick shithouse." Milo hesitated only a moment before trailing his palms over Renner's pecs, watching his nipples stiffen. All of him stiffen, down to his concrete-slab abs and thick, corded arms. "Those shoulders are only a preview, aren't they?"

"Is this your roundabout way of saying I'm attractive?"

"Nothing roundabout about it. You're a dime." Milo dropped his hands to Renner's belt, unfastening it and letting the buckle sag to one side. Then he set to work on the button and zipper, nearly swallowing his tongue when his knuckles brushed the huge bulge waiting on the other side. "Maybe I should start calling *you* pretty boy instead."

Renner's mouth twitched, but his breath was starting to grow stuttered. "I wouldn't recommend it."

Milo pushed the pants down over Renner's hips and shrugged. "Concessions, right?"

"Get on the bed, Milo."

"Loud and clear."

Milo sat down on the edge of the bed, but only had a second to marvel over the ridiculously soft mattress before Renner took his shoulders and pushed him flat on his back. It was familiar, that position. He'd been there countless times, his body ready to give. But there was something different about Renner putting Milo on his back.

Renner came with him.

He paused with his mouth just above Milo's, both of them groaning while Renner locked their hips into a tight position and thrust. Once. Right *there*. "Oh *fuck*," Milo moaned, making a grab for Renner's ass just as the kiss started. And it didn't just start, it took off like a fired bullet. One of Renner's hands took a fistful of Milo's hair and held him steady while he devoured, using his tongue to lap up the harsh, hungry sounds that Milo couldn't seem to contain. His thighs were out of his control, too, riding up Renner's hips, sliding back down, while the man used and abused his mouth like it had been begging for disrespect.

Had it been? Who cares. Disrespect me. Just don't stop.

"Tell me what you think about," Renner demanded, pulling away. Hair had fallen over his forehead and along with that furrowed brow, he looked like a dirty, medieval lord of the manor. "When you think of being with a man—"

"When I think of being with you." Milo pushed back Renner's runaway hair, but it fell right back into the same position. "You, boss man."

"Me, then," Renner murmured, after a moment. "How do you imagine…us?"

Milo had kept the words locked down deep for a long time, but the chain was broken, and nothing would be contained. Nothing would stay inside. "Sometimes I think of you naked and laid out and you're just letting me…touch. Or lick. Whatever and however I want. But it's…"

"What?"

"It's understood that I'm on borrowed time." Milo swallowed a sharp groan when Renner dragged the thick ridge of his cock against Milo's. "Because you want me a certain way and you—"

"I get what I want," Renner finished, his tone heavy. Full. "I already let you borrow time once today. Remember that? When you got on your knees and swallowed me down?"

Milo's eyelids fell and he arched his back. "Hell yeah I remember."

"You liked it. That's good." Milo's eyes flew open when he felt Renner's mouth traveling a path down his chest. Another new sensation. Stubble and…weight. *Perfect.* "Sometimes what I want is exactly what *you* need, Milo." When he was mouth level with Milo's cock, Renner fisted the aching flesh, brushing the head with his lips. "You're going to love learning that lesson."

The head of his erection vanishing into Renner's mouth was the last thing Milo remembered before the struggle set in. The struggle not to come. He shouted something strangled and unintelligible at the ceiling, his hands flying over his head to clutch the slatted headboard. So much room inside Renner's mouth. Almost...too much? Were men's mouths always larger, or was it just this man? He didn't know, but there wasn't an inch of him left out of the warm, hungry suck Renner was giving him. And that's what made his balls wrench tight like they needed to empty themselves fast, because he'd never felt anything like Renner between his thighs.

"Slow..." Milo heaved a jagged breath. "Down."

He looked down at Renner...and realized the man was just as lost to the moment, his eyes shut tight, his cheeks hollow. Just as Milo had been while kneeling on the office floor. Getting pleasure from giving pleasure. Those ridiculous shoulders flexed in the dim light, moving in time with the wet, sucking sounds. Milo's own abdomen hollowed and rebounded like a trampoline, his hips pumping toward the most incredible mouth job of his life. It was dangerous to speed his release like that, but his body seriously didn't give a shit.

"It feels too good, Renner...I can't." A small amount of liquid escaped from his tip and Milo hissed a breath between his teeth. "Stop. *Stop*. I'm going to come."

Renner let his pulsing cock go with an expression that was half satisfied, half hungry for more. He was nothing short of breathtaking, his solid body covered in a light sheen of perspiration, his shined-up lips catching the light. "Fuck, I want to taste what you give up to your first man so bad." He prowled up Milo's body, his cock straining against his stomach. Milo thought he was coming in for a kiss, but he stopped and reached for the nightstand, opening the drawer and taking out a clear bottle. "There'll be time for tasting, though. A lot of it, because your cock hits my throat like a dirty fuck dream. So thick and excited for what it's been dreaming about. I can already hear the sound of your security belt hitting my desk while I yank your pants down around your knees."

Milo reached down and fisted his balls, breathing deeply through his nose so he wouldn't come. "Too much. Too damn much."

Renner leaned down and kissed Milo, twining their tongues together in a slow, comforting kiss that didn't remain that way for long. By the time Renner broke away, Milo was stroking himself off, his stomach and chest heavy with a multitude of weights and emotions. "Tomorrow, you're going to have a very different idea of too much," Renner rasped, sliding his hand beneath Milo's ass. His fingers pressed at the entrance…and they were wet. Really wet. When had that happened? "Say you want it."

"I want it," Milo growled, zero ability to regulate his tone. "You know I do."

With the words still lighting up the air, Renner's mouth closed over Milo's again…and his fingers slid deep. *"Mine."*

Chapter Eighteen

Mine.

Renner had never been so certain of anything in his life. Inside his chest, his heart was roaring like an engine. There was no way to achieve detachment here. Had there ever been a way with Milo? No...no. Since the beginning, he'd been affected, and now he'd sunk down into quicksand. He didn't want to be rescued, either. There might have been a buzzing going off in the back of his mind, warning him to hold back, but it wouldn't be now. It wouldn't be physically, because Renner flat-out wasn't capable of not giving Milo everything inside him. All the words and emotions he'd kept locked away from everyone else.

Milo shuddered beneath him, his mouth falling open with a sound of pleasure/pain. Renner's fingers moved in and out, pushing farther with each stroke, and all the while, Renner split time between kissing Milo's sexy mouth and watching his ink-covered body writhe and flex in the muted light. It took a huge reserve of willpower not to wrestle the man onto his stomach and fuck him through the goddamn headboard. Or hell…maybe keeping him on his back and looking him in the eye. That would be a first, wouldn't it?

One that made his pulse pick up speed.

Milo wanted it on his stomach, though. He'd said so. Did that mean he was hesitant to be so intimate, so soon?

"Renner…" Milo's hand slipping up his chest snapped him out of his head. "Feels good…it's starting to feel so good."

Christ, the vision of Milo's half-mast eyes, his mouth opening to release slurred words, his plump cock lying across his belly…it burned itself into Renner's memory. Nothing hotter. Nothing better. *No one I want or need more.*

The continued realization that he'd fallen *hard* for the security guard had Renner reeling more than a little bit. But Milo's increasing groans and pumping hips had him throwing his mental bullshit on the back burner. Carefully, he drew his fingers out of Milo, unable to stop himself from leaning down and taking a long, rough suck of Milo's swollen cock, groaning when a touch of saltiness coated his tongue. Between his legs, his own flesh was weighed down and miserable with the need to rock into Milo's tight ass. Rock and rock. A pounding started in his temples, his blood heating until Renner could actually feel it flowing.

His rasping breath punctuating the air, Renner reached for the bedside table once again and closed his fist around a condom packet. His gaze clashed with Milo's, and he could see what the other man wanted. What he needed. And that he was tasking Renner with giving it to him.

Biting down on the condom between his teeth, Renner slid two hands beneath Milo's hips and flipped him over on the bed, both of them moaning at the rightness of the position. The rightness for them. Light and shadow played across Milo's splayed back, shifting as he grabbed on to the headboard. There was no choice but for Renner to take a moment to appreciate the work of art underneath him, because doing otherwise would have been tragic.

He conformed his palms to the smooth roundness of Milo's bottom, running his thumb through the split down the middle. "You think I would have let someone else take this home?" Watching Milo's knuckles go white on the headboard with expectancy, Renner reared back with his right hand and slapped it across the waiting flesh. "You think I would have risked you not being given every goddamn thing you need?"

Another biting spank.

"No…" Milo breathed, his shoulders heaving. "I don't know. You tell me."

A sharp pain hit Renner between the ribs as he rolled the condom down his cock. "Don't worry, I'm about to make it really clear who the fuck you go home with." His mouth was begging for the salty smooth texture of Milo's skin, so Renner dropped forward and allowed his tongue to lick pathways up Milo's neck, down between his shoulder blades, and up his spine. He was almost too distracted by Milo's harsh curses to use the bottle in his hand, but he knew how necessary it was. With the slick glide sufficient enough, Renner gripped his cock with a grunt and slid it between Milo's cheeks, riding the warm curves with desperate surges of his hips.

Milo punched the headboard with a choked rendition of Renner's name. "Don't stop doing that. Please. I love it."

Renner's laugh was agonized and full of lust. He wasn't even inside Milo yet and his reactions were off the charts, his buttocks flexing, voice straining. A man didn't stand a chance against Milo's brand of honesty—it was sexy and gut-wrenchingly beautiful at the same time. And it belonged to him, goddammit. Didn't it? Yes. *Yes.*

The rush of possessiveness had Renner jerking Milo's hips off the bed, grinding that lube-slicked ass into his lap. "Show me how you would have danced with me tonight." He thrust so hard Milo was forced to catch himself on the pillows, the material clutched between his fingers. "Get the other men touching you out of my head. Do it now."

Renner added Milo's ability to adapt and rise to any occasion to the list of things Renner loved about him, because the man pushed his knees wider on the bedspread. No hesitation, except maybe the second he paused to groan into the mattress. Both of their breathing racing out of control, sweat forming between their bodies, Milo moved his backside in a figure eight, dragging Renner's stiff cock along with him. "Like that, Renner?" His back rolled, shoulders to waist, like wake from a boat. "You could have been out there with me. All you had to do was demand it."

Shit. He was losing his composure here. Milo was giving him a lap dance from his hands and knees, though, and who the fuck could keep a thought in their head with that happening? His hand moved on its own, traveling around the bumping rhythm of Milo's hips to jerk him off…and damn it if the torture didn't only increase, Milo's body grinding back on Renner's dick. And then Milo had the nerve to look back over his shoulder—all heavy-lidded and ready to submit— making it impossible for Renner to wait another second. There was a wire connecting every aching erogenous zone below his waist and it grew hotter and tighter every time the man beneath him popped his hips. Like a trained entertainer who'd been working it for the wrong crowd all along. Renner needed inside Milo *now* or he would lose his mind.

He lunged forward, flattening Milo on the bed, wedging his mouth up against the panting man's ear. "There's a limit to what I could stand from you in public, Milo. That's your second lesson tonight. You put your ass in *my* lap and this is what happens." He fisted his erection and guided it through Milo's glossed ass cheeks, stopping right where he needed it to go. So damn bad. "Relax, baby."

The endearment was unexpected, but Renner would have

died before taking it back. Especially when Milo's response was to slide his left hand back. Reaching for Renner's.

Renner stared for a moment, heart hammering in his throat, before twining his fingers with Milo's and squeezing his hand tight. The craving for even more closeness with this man became undeniable after that. Renner pressed his stomach and chest to Milo's spine, burying his open mouth against his neck...and pushed his cock halfway home, hot friction wrapping around his flesh and throttling it. A fist pushed low in his belly and twisted, making the urge to come almost unbearable. His blood surged with the claim he was making, the dominance of it, the responsibility of being the first.

"Fuck," Milo breathed, his back bunching into knots beneath Renner. "Okay, okay."

Renner choked on an inhale and beat back the simultaneous urge to plow forward and pull out, to stop Milo from experiencing any pain. Their hands were so tightly clasped, they were both probably going to lose circulation. Worth it, though. *Worth it.* He could feel every wince and draw of breath from Milo, as if it were coming from his own body. And maybe that kind of connection with another person should have scared him, but nothing was scarier than stopping. Not being there when Milo experienced the completion to come. Being the *reason* for it.

"Try to..." Renner closed his eyes and licked the patch of skin beneath Milo's ear, attempting to center himself, even though his dick was pulsing, begging to ram deeper into the constricted space between Milo's ass cheeks. To shove those cheeks wide and watch himself tunnel into that slippery, untested entrance. "Try to breathe. Try to relax."

"I could tell you the same thing." Milo laughed into the pillow, but it turned into a groan. "It feels bad and good at the same time."

Yeah. Renner knew the feeling. "This isn't borrowed time, Milo. We're on *your* time right now." He reached for the bottle he'd discarded near his thigh and slid it between them, applying more of the liquid, gritting his teeth as the moisture coasted and dripped around their joined bodies. *Need to move. Need to come.* "I want to spread you open and pump until I can't see straight, but I'm not moving until you ask for it."

"Well, when you say things like that…"

They both laughed, but it was strained with lust. And something else.

It was the sound of a bond being cemented.

"Tell me more about how it feels for you," Milo said. "I…I think this thing inside me that likes to make you happy…it does something to take away the pain."

I could love this man.

I could love him forever.

Maybe I already do.

"You—" Renner heard the emotion in his voice and worked to stabilize it. "You were weird about coming into this place? Like maybe you didn't belong?" He pushed a kiss into Milo's neck, stroking the spot with his tongue, commanding himself not to thrust into the slightness squeezing the top half of his rigid cock. "I felt like I'd walked in here with the fucking jackpot, baby. You have any idea what you do to me?"

A subtle tilt of Renner's hips made Milo clench around him, sending heat slamming into his tightened-up balls. "I've been watching you, too. Watching you move and laugh and give me attitude for months. Now I'm inside you. Giving you your first fuck." Releasing Milo's hand, Renner wedged his own between Milo's body and the mattress, gripping the man's cock tight. Jesus, it was thick, probably hurting as much as Renner's. "I've never been so hot to get off in my life. Been hot for it all along. Nonstop. And that was before I knew you were going to feel this fucking sweet taking my dick."

Milo's muscles had relaxed in increments while Renner spoke, and now he tilted his hips and ripped a growl from Renner's chest. "More."

A blast of hunger clawed up Renner's spine, and he experienced a head rush of responsibility along with the incredible need. Milo begun pumping his hips into Renner's fist, and there was no holding himself back anymore. Nothing could keep him from thrusting his remaining inches into Milo's tight entry, holding himself deep as Milo shuddered beneath him...shuddered, sucked in a breath, then continued to fuck Renner's fist.

"Oh God," Milo ground out. "*Yes.* More, please. Yes."

Renner didn't need any more encouragement. He planted his free hand on the mattress and let himself go, canting his hips up and back, using that primed asshole to take out his greedy lust. *Fuck*, the texture was so raw, Renner's neck lost power, his jaw going slack at the rough, narrow heat he'd been gifted with. "Yeah, I feel your ass is working up and down against my stomach. Over and over because your cock is so swollen and it needs to fuck my hand." Milo's moans told him it was okay to pump harder and he did, damn near losing his mind over the slap of his heavy sack against Milo's taut cheeks. "I think you're going to be climbing the stairs to my office early and often, aren't you?" He sank his teeth into the meat of Milo's shoulder and listened to his breath stutter and rush in. "'Stop working and ride me, Renner. You broke me in and now I can't think of anything but your cock.' Is that what you'll say?"

"*Yes.*"

Renner nudged Milo's head until he could see his face. There were bloody teeth marks on his lower lip and sweat glistening on his forehead. Signs of struggling that might have worried Renner if the other man's eyes weren't bleary with sex. "God, you are fucking gorgeous," Renner said, his voice shaking, out of his control along with the rest of his body, his muscles quickening with each passing second, preparing for release. *"Gorgeous."*

Milo moved and their mouths connected, lips working together instead of battling, like they'd been doing before. The tinge of blood made the kiss a promise as their lips opened wide, so wide, allowing tongues to sweep in. Tasting, licking, flickering.

That promise of a kiss was what it took for Renner's dam to finally crumble into a heap, and with it, his willpower lost the fight, too. Milo's breath shortened and his body stiffened, especially his rounded, sweat-slicked, clenching backside, words chanting from his mouth that translated into *I'm coming, Renner.* Renner understood him perfectly, because Milo's closing up around his cock made his own release pulverize him seconds later. He sank deep, so deep, into Milo's undulating body as their tongues did the same and rode the thunderheads.

They didn't move right away when the sweat began to cool moments later, as if both of them were wary of the magic dissipating. But it didn't. And when Renner pulled Milo into the crook of his neck and heard his breath go heavy with sleep, Renner was so sure nothing *could* take away the magic.

But fate had a funny way of proving one wrong.

Chapter Nineteen

Milo woke up with a sense of impending doom.

He didn't know where it came from. Hadn't felt anything like it since he'd been overseas and woken to the sound of blasts in the distance. Or heard a fellow soldier fighting off demons on the middle of the night. This was a different kind of doom, though. It wasn't something he could pinpoint, but he somehow knew the day would end much differently than last night.

Last night.

Milo blew out a breath and opened his eyes, well aware that Renner wouldn't be lying beside him. When they'd walked into the bedroom the night before, his surroundings had been the furthest thing from his mind. He explored the sunlit space now through fresh eyes and felt the pit in his stomach yawn wider.

There was a fucking *chandelier* over the bed.

Turning his head toward the window, he felt the rasp of silk beneath his neck and wished—wished like hell—Renner had stayed in bed. His presence would have guaranteed Milo wouldn't think of anything else. Like how high the rent on the apartment must be. Wait, no. It was a co-op, meaning Renner had *bought* the place. Probably paid somewhere near eight figures for it. Tipped the doorman at Christmas and everything.

Okay. Last night this gap in their economic status hadn't been a big deal, and it *still* wasn't this morning. Milo had meant what he said. Maybe the fact that Renner was his boss and could buy and sell him should get under his skin more. Fact was, it didn't. Renner's power and influence were secondary to how he felt about the actual man himself, but they were still a turn-on. *My boyfriend is a big deal and he* earned *that right, so kiss my ass.*

Would he ever have the chance to say those words? Honest to God, Milo didn't know. Because while their differences weren't a deal breaker for Milo, he wondered if they might be for Renner. Was a security guard enough for him? What would happen if they decided to be together? Would Milo just sit around and wait for Renner's monthly drop-in to the factory?

Panic had Milo sitting up in bed, looking out through the pristine window toward New Jersey, which wasn't visible so far east, but he knew it lay just on the other side of the Hudson. He lifted a hand to massage the stiffness from his neck. It had gotten that way from using Renner's shoulder as a pillow, and he wouldn't trade the sore muscles for anything. Not a damn thing.

You and Renner are together now. You'll figure everything out one fight at a time.

No other options.

Because his feelings for the man who'd left him alone in the bed? They were real. They were raw and new and scary… and they weren't going anywhere. When he'd met Travis, his attraction to the chef had almost been born of curiosity. *Holy shit, those images I've been substituting for women weren't a mistake. I can't ignore them now that I'm attracted to a specific man.* He'd almost felt more...*grateful* to Travis than anything. For not giving him the option of hiding anymore. When he thought of the perpetually smiling blond now, his memories were fond, but they didn't make his palms sweat. They didn't make his pulse go wild.

Not like Renner. Strong, stubborn, secretive Renner.

Intuition—or maybe the empty side of the bed—told Milo he had a battle on his hands. Right now. This morning. Over money, geography, maybe even their age difference...he didn't know. And he didn't give a fuck, either.

Milo swung his legs over the side of the bed to go find out what he had to beat.

• • •

Renner was about to make a monumental mistake.

But he'd opened his eyes this morning knowing it was inevitable.

Without bothering to put on a shirt, Renner had snagged a pair of boxers from the dresser drawer and left Milo sleeping in his bed. Not without stopping and staring at the mess of Milo's dark hair on his pillow, the tattooed muscles sprawled in four directions, for longer than he would admit out loud, because it would make him a creeper.

Milo. Goddammit, he was a sight first thing in the morning. If waking up with that man in his arms was something that could be procured with money, life would be so much easier, wouldn't it? But Milo could belong to Renner only if he paid a very different kind of fee. He had to hand over his heart. Maybe somewhere in the darkness last night, Renner had already offered it to him. Only in pieces, though. With qualifications.

And Milo deserved better. He deserved an intact heart.

Unfortunately, there was something preventing Renner from taking that leap. It had been in the back of his mind during every single interaction with Milo, taunting him, lying in wait to rattle him at inopportune moments. The only way to combat the worry was to fight it head-on. Which, of course, was a huge mistake. One that he'd been destined to make.

Renner set down his cup of coffee on the kitchen counter, hesitated for a split second, then booted his laptop. He watched the display appear, the icons growing more distinct along with the dread in his chest. Dousing it with coffee didn't work, only making the sick feeling worse. So he ripped off the Band-Aid, hating himself all the while.

Opening the browser, he searched the words: "Travis, celebrity chef."

There he was.

Renner's stomach dropped.

You shouldn't have looked.

Jesus, the guy could have been Renner's college boyfriend. Or the identical rowing teammate for whom he'd blown off Renner. Sure, there were differences. The chef looked more down-to-earth. More comfortable in his own skin than any college student. His hair was shaggy, his flannel shirt casual. The similarities were what caught Renner right in the chin, though. Happy. The guy was so damn happy in every picture Renner scrolled past. Smiling while he chopped some cilantro or squeezed a lime. A lot like Milo.

Perfect for Milo.

Young, optimistic, charismatic. Married to his job, but clearly finding time to live life. Travis was a rock climbing, karaoke singing, fashion show attending motherfucker. Renner hated him. Because he could offer Milo a place to flourish. A place to finally be himself with a boyfriend who didn't fight him on everything or spend countless hours working. A boyfriend who didn't already have a heart condition at the age of thirty-three.

Renner must have been a secret glutton for punishment, because although a voice screamed in the back of his mind to shut the laptop, he hit play on a video of Travis instead.

Australian? The fucking guy was *Australian*?

"What are you doing?" Milo said from his bedroom doorway. "Renner. What the hell?"

Pressure pushing from all sides in his throat, Renner slammed the laptop shut and drank a mouthful of coffee, the liquid burning all the way down. "Good morning, Milo."

A dark eyebrow went up. "I think you know where to shove that good morning."

Milo was tense as he walked from the bedroom, wearing only a pair of gray briefs. And more than a little outrage. Which didn't stop Renner from getting hard behind the kitchen counter, because the man was bed-tousled and messy. Now was not the time to think of messing him up even further, but Renner couldn't stop himself. Their sex last night couldn't even be described with words, it had been so...raw. They'd been the only two people in the universe. But Renner had just allowed in one more, hadn't he?

Hip cocked, eyes on fire, Milo jabbed a finger in his direction. "You better not be thinking about fucking right now." Panic laced into his expression as he looked between Renner and the laptop. "Not after that. *Why*, Renner?"

"I had to know." It sounded stupid when voiced out loud, of course, and Milo's humorless smirk confirmed that fact. Renner could feel his knee-jerk reaction rising to the surface. Could feel the defensiveness taking over. But he was too fucked up over witnessing the glory of Australian Rock Climbing Travis to keep it leashed. "Don't act like this was some huge betrayal on my part, Milo. You came to me asking for help in talking to this guy. *Asking him out.* If the roles were reversed, you would have done the same thing." Renner flattened a hand on the laptop. "He's the reason we started spending time together and he's been here all along, so don't *come* at me like this."

The tension leached from Milo's body, his expression losing about 90 percent of its anger. Softening in a way that made Renner want to start the morning from scratch. "Okay. Yeah. You know what, you're right." Renner had barely recovered from his shock when Milo continued. "I'm sorry. I thought…I thought you would realize it was you and me now. He wasn't in the picture anymore until you brought him in."

Renner ignored the blast of relief. "Look, I don't have an easy time trusting men."

"Why?"

Nails raked down the back of Renner's neck. He didn't want to talk about the past or how it had crippled him. Not to this man, who'd so bravely entered a new world and never looked back. It was humiliating. It would change the way Milo looked at him, and Renner couldn't stand the prospect of that happening.

Instead of honesty, instead of keeping down the wall they'd worked so hard to crumble, Renner did the opposite. He built an even higher barrier and flew an idiot flag from the parapet.

"I need you to go to Boston." The words were like broken glass coming out of his mouth. "I need you to go meet with Travis as planned and make sure there's nothing there."

Milo rocked back on his heels, a hand reaching to the couch for balance. *"What?"*

"Please don't make me say it again."

Heavy silence passed. "If it was so hard to say it, why do it at all?"

Renner didn't have an answer to that. It was too logical when set against a world where Milo eventually decided someone else was a better option. Better options were everywhere. Not just in Boston. They were on the internet and in clubs, waiting to swoop in the second Renner turned his back. "I'll be in Hook when you come back. If you still want me there."

Apparently Milo had been keeping himself in check, because as soon as those words were out of Renner's mouth, his chest started to shudder up and down with agitated breaths. "I don't know a lot about relationships. With men *or* women. But I know this relationship you and I have…it doesn't work if you keep letting me go. We *agreed* on this last night. Even if you have your reasons. All you're doing is making me less and less secure." His throat worked. "Eventually I'm going to wonder if you want me around at all."

"Milo." They waited. But Renner didn't speak. What was there to say? *Stay?* The fucking worry wasn't going anywhere. Tomorrow morning he'd be back to wondering when Milo would start considering his options and looking for the escape hatch. "I'm the first man you've been with. It's normal to feel a strong attachment—"

"Stop. Just stop. The attachment was there before we ever touched." While Renner was forced to acknowledge the truth of that statement, Milo lifted a tense shoulder and let it fall. "Tell me to stay. Tell me you can't stand the idea of me with someone else. Please."

Cymbals crashed inside Renner's head, but nothing came out of his mouth. All he could see was Milo breaking up with him in some coffee shop, while Travis waited impatiently in the corner.

"Okay." Milo laughed, but it was empty of humor. "I guess we're done here."

Milo spun on a heel and disappeared into the bedroom. Renner fought the tug-of-war with two impulses. Go to him, pin him to the bed, and apologize until his voice gave out.

Or let him go and stand firm on what he believed was the right decision. It *was*. If Milo came back from Boston, having decided he was really no longer interested in Travis, they would build on a more solid foundation. One Renner could be sure of.

He was feeling the opposite of sure when Milo breezed past, dressed in the clothes he'd worn last night, smelling like Renner's bed. Before he could reach the door, Milo stopped and addressed Renner. "I can forgive you for being insecure over Travis. That's on me, okay? I'm sorry he was the reason I used to get close to you. Because now I know that's what I really wanted all along."

The floor turned to water under Renner's feet. "Jesus, Milo—"

"But I can't forgive you for telling me I don't know my own mind." He twisted the dead bolt on the door and wrenched it open. "I spent too damn long not sure of myself and I'm done. I know who I am and what I want. I'm going to Boston to prove that to myself. Not you." Milo took one step out the door and paused without looking back. "Don't forget to take your heart pills."

When the door closed, it took several moments for Renner to move. And when he did, it was only to slide down to the floor, where he stayed, trying to breathe through the agony.

Chapter Twenty

Milo had worn the stupid jacket for his dinner with Travis just to be defiant.

Or maybe he'd worn it to feel close to Renner, the prick.

Yeah. He wasn't sure of his reasoning regarding the fake leather outerwear from hell. There was no way to be positive of *anything* when your heart was a mangled mess. You simply got up, dressed yourself, and kept moving. Right? You didn't get to sleep in on the morning after combat. A solider woke up to the sound of his alarm, shined his fucking boots, and got ready to do it all over again. Bleeding battle wounds be damned.

After taking the train back to Hook, he'd hit the ground running by packing for his trip to Boston. If he'd stopped to think about Renner sending him off to another man after the night they'd spent together, he might not see the mission through. And Milo was determined. As he'd said to Renner on his way out the door, he wasn't having dinner with Travis to prove to Renner his feelings were genuine. No. This was about believing in himself after years of questions.

He was in love with Renner Bastion, and his date with Travis could be a five-star night with belly dancers, fireworks, and a roasted pig—nothing was changing his mind.

Milo waited for the busy Boston intersection to clear, then started across the street toward the restaurant where Travis would be. With every step Milo took, he felt worse. Felt like dying, actually. His air passages were thinner, his blood cold. *Renner, you fucker.* Just like being in the club last night, he'd been abandoned. Treated carelessly. And it went against everything he needed from Renner. This connection between them relied on Renner being possessive and yeah, maybe a little controlling. It depended upon Milo being loyal to a fault.

All of this. *All of it* was wrong.

How ridiculous that he was scanning the street for Renner. How embarrassingly naive. But Milo ached down to the soles of his feet to see that big, suited figure striding down the sidewalk, putting a halt to Milo's progress into the restaurant. *Come on. Come through.*

Milo waited a full count to ten with his hand on the entrance door, before giving up and walking inside.

• • •

Five hours earlier

Renner stared at the glow of his office computer screen in disbelief.

It had worked. Milo's plan to land the account had worked.

After firing off proposals to several of Rocky Mountain Ltd.'s competitors, Renner now had an email from the CEO saying they were reconsidering their relationship with their current manufacturer and wanted to meet with Renner in person. Which was a foot in the door and in Renner's case, as good as a signed deal. He never walked out of a boardroom with anything less.

Apart from the computer screen, there wasn't a single light on in the factory, because it was a Saturday. The darkness was fitting. It matched Renner's insides. His Milo was on the way to Boston for a date with another man. Rendering the email in front of him entirely meaningless. Who cared? Who cared about anything but the man who'd slept in his arms last night? Without Milo to celebrate the victory with, it was empty. A void. Silent.

Was Milo laughing right now? Was he glad he'd gone?

Renner stood and plowed his fist into the wall, feeling one of his knuckles pop. Pain shot up his arm, but it was welcome. Thank *God* for the pain. Only it didn't last. It sailed away too fast, replaced by the feel of Milo holding his hand in the darkness.

"*Fuck*," Renner roared, then louder. "*Fuck!*"

Without registering his intent, Renner sat down at the computer and started to respond to the email, blood trickling down his wrist, dripping onto the keyboard.

He was rejecting the meeting. Turning it down flat. He didn't want to be in business with a company who judged a corporation based on his private life, and not on its track record.

As soon as Renner made the decision, a valve in his chest turned and pressure released. How long had he been living with the strain without realizing it wasn't normal? Too long. All this time, he'd thought earning the account was about proving he could operate in every aspect of the manufacturing world. Now that the moment arrived...he realized the industry needed to adapt to *him*. Not the other way around. He was damn good at his job and wouldn't make any compromises. He worked harder than anyone. And this final step, this final area where he'd thought proving himself was necessary? Turned out, it wasn't.

He'd already done that.

And yeah, it was his imagination, but Milo's voice found him in the darkness, right against his ear. *Score one for the boss man.*

Hearing it was the final push Renner needed to hit send on the email. Hell, Milo had been pushing him all along, hadn't he? Believing in Renner when he didn't believe in himself. Forcing him to acknowledge his accomplishments. Why hadn't he listened? Instead, his insecurities had been a noose around the neck of their relationship, robbing it of breath before it could even get started. Renner's lack of confidence in himself as a businessman had only been the brick portion of the wall he'd built. The mortar had oozed out in the form of jealousy.

Pointless, baseless jealousy and distrust of the *one person* who'd refused to give up on him, no matter how mean or condescending he acted. The man who'd had his back for months, never once deterred in his determination to be Renner's friend. To be more. Until now.

Eventually I'm going to wonder if you want me around at all.

"Christ," Renner rasped, pushing to his feet and searching the surface of his desk for car keys. *Have to get to Boston. Have to get there.* "Jesus *Christ.*"

Without bothering to shut down his computer, Renner blew down the stairs to the factory floor and made for the side exit, which led into the employee parking lot. He'd parked there to make Milo happy, but his boyfriend would never know, would he? Milo was on some quest to stop Renner from questioning his loyalty, when questioning it was the one thing that could inflict damage.

Was it too late to patch the wound?

Please God, don't let me be too late.

• • •

Milo looked across the table at Travis.

It was like standing beneath a sprinkle when he'd just fought to the surface of a tidal wave. The dampness barely registered. At one time, he'd been magnetized by Travis. Hadn't he? Or had being with Renner erased his sense memory? He felt nothing for Travis now but fondness. But he'd already known that before the drive to Boston, so that acknowledgment didn't surprise him at all. God he was numb.

Travis laughed into the uncomfortable silence. "I was glad you called," the chef said. "You left Boston without any notice. I wondered if there was some kind of family emergency."

"No." Milo's voice sounded rusty, so he cleared it, but the effort only made his chest ache more. "No, some army buddies had a security gig for me. I guess I was looking for a change of scenery, too."

"Oh, and a pop star wasn't good enough scenery?" Travis teased, waggling his eyebrows. "This security gig must be pretty sweet to leave Holly Burbank behind."

When he'd pictured this dinner, it hadn't been easy. Throw in the added weight of heartbreak, and everything was distorted and hollow. He just wanted to be anywhere else. *Anywhere*. Or maybe just drunk to the point of forgetting the taste of Renner's mouth. The anchor of his hands when they fisted in Milo's hair. His elusive laugh.

He wouldn't allow this opportunity to pass, though. As much as it hurt to even be functioning in a humanlike capacity right now, Milo owed it to himself to make the most of this dinner. Maybe the outcome would be far different than he'd ever imagined, but it would have a purpose. It wouldn't be wasted on self-pity.

"I, um…" Milo picked up his beer and set it back down. "It *is* a pretty sweet gig. Back in New Jersey. I wasn't sure if everything would feel the same, with those friends from the army. We weren't fighting and away from home anymore. But it's actually better. They're good people. There are so many *good* people in Hook."

Travis's eyebrows drew together, clearly puzzled by the serious turn in conversation. "Glad to hear it, man."

"Yeah. I'm going back. I'm happy there." Nerves whizzed in Milo's bloodstream. Not the excited type he experienced around Renner. Just general, *holy shit I'm talking openly about things that used to be a mystery* kind of nerves. "I'm actually in Boston tonight to see you. Specifically."

"Really?" Travis leaned forward, elbows on the table. "Why?"

"Well. Mostly because I'm in love with this jerk and he's blowing it."

The chef did a double take. "Come again?" He pointed at Milo. "You're—"

"Yeah." He nodded once, enjoying the rush of freedom. "Yes."

"Oh." Travis's mouth tugged at one side. "Well, I guess that explains why you could give up the job watching Holly's back so easily."

Milo laughed. "Yeah. Something like that." He drummed his fingers on the table. "Anyway, I just wanted to tell you it helped me a lot…watching how confident you were in being… you. It went a long way toward me doing the same."

"Wow. I don't know what to say," Travis said, running a hand through his blond hair. "You're welcome and let's celebrate? Take your mind off the jerk for a while?"

As if anything would.

"Sounds good."

Milo sat back and listened to Travis talk about his experiences cooking for several celebrities and one blooper he'd taken credit for on the *Today* show. In fact, Milo didn't say much at all, and he was kind of grateful Travis apparently talked a lot more than he remembered.

It gave Milo time to think.

After what he'd said to Travis about learning to be himself, Milo needed to put his money where his mouth was. He'd always been the kind of man who forgave easily. It was just his nature. But he wouldn't go back to Hook and pick up where he'd left off with Renner, even though he'd proven his feelings for Travis were purely friendly.

No, that wouldn't work. He'd been hurt. Not just his heart, but his pride, had been scored. Letting Renner back in while his wounds were still fresh would guarantee he healed with mangled scar tissue, instead of a clean scar.

Milo couldn't let that happen. Maybe the Milo who'd followed Renner around for months, trying to learn from his confidence, would have smiled through the pain of being cut loose. *Again.* But Milo was worth more than that. He was worthy of *better.* Always had been, despite his lack of money. It shouldn't have taken his broken heart to force that realization, but sometimes an old idea needed to burn down for a better one to be built on top. Over the past week, he'd come out to his friends, thrown himself into new situations, and driven to Boston, facing the past insecurities he'd run away from. He wasn't hiding anymore, and he wouldn't be cast aside, either. Allowing someone to do that to him only damaged the progress he'd made.

As brutally difficult as it would be, he needed to steer clear of Renner Bastion until his newfound convictions took a permanent hold. Because he wouldn't survive being pushed away or cast aside ever again. Hell, he wasn't even sure he'd survive it this time.

• • •

Renner had hit traffic.

The shitty kind that didn't cooperate no matter how many

times a man laid on the horn or made promises to God. And the second Milo stepped out of the restaurant—wearing that goddamn jacket—Renner had the overwhelming sense that he'd lost him.

From across the street, Renner watched as he shook hands with the Australian chef, each of them going his separate way. Which should have been a relief, but wasn't, because Renner had already gut-checked himself into knowing the connection between him and Milo ran both ways. That it was authentic and something to be treasured, not handled so fucking callously that Renner could barely stomach thinking about what he'd done.

Watching as Milo shoved his hands into his jeans pockets, trudging down the street alone, Renner made a low sound and crossed the street after him.

"*Milo,*" Renner called, just as he reached the sidewalk. "Milo."

The other man stopped and turned...and it was right there on his face. The proof that Renner had come way too late to save the day. That closed-off expression pummeled him like a heavyweight boxer, because he'd never seen Milo anything but open. Without barriers.

Jesus, if I don't fix this, I'll never recover. Never forgive myself.

"I'm sorry." Renner approached Milo slowly, his voice cutting through the traffic racing past. "I can't believe I asked you to come here. I'm...ashamed I even thought about it."

Milo looked away. "Why?"

They were only a few yards apart now, and Renner wanted to lunge the remaining distance and drag Milo into his arms, but knew it would be too much. Worse, he might lose this chance to explain himself. To *look* at Milo and *talk* to him. "Why?" Renner sucked up his fears and spoke from the middle of his chest. "Because you are mine, Milo. I'm yours. And I shouldn't have questioned that. I *hate* myself for questioning that."

He'd surprised Milo. Thank God. Surprised the shut-down expression off his face by being the one to say the words out loud. "How do I know—" He halted midsentence and ripped the jacket off his body, hurling it at the closest trash can. "I hate that fucking jacket."

Renner's heart seized. "Yeah. I hate it, too."

Milo pinched the bridge of his nose, visibly trying to calm down, and it was a huge relief, knowing he wasn't calm. Because Renner was a zillion miles from anything *resembling* calm. The date was over. The buzzer had gone off and he'd failed. Renner knew how god-awful sitting in traffic had been, wanting to claw off his own skin. But what had it been like for *Milo*? To be in the actual restaurant, thinking Renner didn't give enough of a fuck to stop him?

"What were you going to say?" Renner rasped.

"How do I know you won't *do* this again?" Milo burst out. "Fuck you, Renner. This *hurt*."

Renner was winded by the pain in Milo's voice. "I'm sorry."

"Aren't you going to ask me how it went?" Milo asked, coming closer and shoving one of Renner's shoulders. Renner welcomed it, because at least Milo was touching him. "Aren't you going to ask if there's going to be a second date?"

"No, I'm not," Renner managed around the misery of the very possibility. "You're coming back to Hook because you told me you would. You said it and I believe you. And because I'm not leaving without my boyfriend."

Milo's eyes flickered at Renner's use of the title, but they cut away. "You are, actually." He stepped back. Away. "I'm making my own way home. I need some time."

"I need *you*." Renner had no choice but to lay himself bare. "Milo, I…there was someone who hurt me a long time ago. It was serious. And he left me for someone else." Funny how making the admission now was so easy. So easy, but so late. A face from the past had no place in that moment when the present world was ending. "That doesn't give me the right to assume you would do the same. I know that. I think I tried to push you into it because…you leaving me was inevitable."

"It wasn't," Milo whispered, giving a jerky shrug of his shoulders. "It was you since the beginning."

"It's me now." Renner stepped closer. "Can you just let it be me now?"

Milo backed away, looking torn. Confused. "I don't know anymore." It clearly hurt him to say those words, but he wasn't taking them back. Strength was bleeding through the confusion, and it was nothing short of beautiful. Agonizing but beautiful. "I *claimed* you, Renner. I made you my friend. Made you my…more. I needed you to claim me in return. That was *all* I needed."

Renner could barely speak around the failure, but he couldn't let Milo leave without making him a vow. Something to remember. "I'm not giving up on us. I'm not going away," Renner ground out, repeating back Milo's words from a long-ago day in his office. "I'm *refusing* to be without you."

I love you.

If Renner had said it out loud, maybe Milo would have stayed, instead of turning the corner and vanishing out of sight, leaving Renner reeling on the sidewalk.

Chapter Twenty-One

So this is what is feels like to be a zombie.

Renner could barely muster the energy it took to move the gearshift, putting his car into park. After that, he could only stare through the windshield at the cinder-block exterior of the factory, breathing. He'd taken the final available space in the employee parking lot, which was new, since he was usually the first to arrive. Cutting himself some slack when it came to work had become easier, though, for two reasons. Because of Milo, Renner had finally stepped back and taken stock of his accomplishments and realized he no longer needed to grind himself into the ground to achieve his version of success. And secondly, work had fallen to number two on the list of important things.

Number one was probably inside the factory wondering if Renner still cared.

Still cared? He was *consumed*. Some moments he wondered if he would ever be capable of caring about anything but the man who owned his heart.

Staying away had been like sawing off his limbs with

a rusted blade, but Renner hadn't laid eyes on Milo in five miserable days. Now he leaned back against the headrest and closed his eyes. Not grinding himself into the ground. Right. Is that why he'd been working late every night this week?

It would be worth turning into a flesh-eating half human if his efforts won back Milo. He was doing it the only way he knew how. Through being business-minded. Through being... Renner. Maybe if he'd stayed true to himself when it came to Milo, he wouldn't be in such physical pain right now. Did he even have the wherewithal to climb out of the car? What if his plan didn't work?

He couldn't just live *without* the best thing that ever happened to him. Did people do that? Was this shitty, aching wasteland in the center of his chest where all the sappy love songs came from? If so, Renner now had a whole new appreciation. Over the last five days, he could have written fifty albums while mourning the loss of the greatest gain imaginable.

Being cut off from Milo hadn't done a damn thing to decrease the possessiveness. His man was alone at night. Renner wasn't there to keep him warm. To keep his body sated. Worse, he knew Milo had a need to fuss over Renner that wasn't being met, tripling his misery. Had he actually complained about Milo bringing him sandwiches? How could a man be so blind to luck?

More than once a day, he'd broken down and called Samantha, asking for news about Milo. God knew his sister had a bleeding heart, but she wasn't taking any mercy on him either, doling out the tiniest tidbits—Milo is alive... Milo looked hot today—before claiming the pregnancy was making her tired. And hanging up.

Winning back the man he loved and needed beyond reason was up to him.

So today he would take his shot. If he failed...

He would live with a hole in his chest. Indefinitely.

His apology in Boston hadn't been enough, so Renner had gone big. At this point, all he had was hope. Hope that Milo hadn't spent the last five days realizing he was better off without Renner. Or assuming Renner had moved on without a fight.

Yeah. Not happening.

A loud knock on the driver's-side window had Renner's spine snapping straight. "What the—" Standing outside the car were Duke and Vaughn, arms crossed, looking prepared to mete out vengeance. Zombie killers. "What do you want?"

Vaughn leaned back against the car parked beside Renner's Mercedes. "You want to get out of the car or what?"

"Not particularly, no." But he was too fucking tired to shout through the glass, so Renner unlocked the door and pulled the handle, nudging it open a few inches. "Shouldn't you be working?"

"We were going to ask you the same question," Duke answered. "You usually break balls around the factory before leaving us to our own devices and going to oversee another project. But the light has been off in your office for days, and you have everyone worried."

Renner had to throw an eye roll at that. "Oh, right. I'm positive every employee is praying the Rosary as we speak, just terrified something happened to their beloved boss." Duke and Vaughn exchanged a look that made Renner anxious. "What? What was that?"

"It's only one employee, really," Vaughn said, shifting in his boots. "Milo is a wreck thinking you left Jersey for good. And while we're on the subject of our friend from Boston…"

"You need to figure that shit out," Duke finished, completely unaware that Renner's heart had rammed into his throat at the mention of Milo being upset. "We don't know what happened between you two—"

"Which is pretty much bullshit, because that's part of the reason we bowl." Duke sniffed. "To figure out romantic—"

"Puzzles," Vaughn finished, using his fingers to demonstrate. "It's like putting together a puzzle. You don't see the full picture until someone adds the right piece."

Renner stared. "Who *are* you people?"

Duke and Vaughn threw up their hands.

"We're your unsolicited reality check, man," Vaughn said, slapping the top of the Mercedes. "Milo is a mess. You're an even *worse* mess, probably because you're the one who fucked up—"

"Couldn't have been Milo." Duke shook his head. "I don't see it having been Milo."

"And it has been five days." Vaughn tapped a finger against his watch. "Take it from someone who knows, the more time you let pass, the worse it's going to get."

Duke made a gruff sound of agreement. Then they both stared at Renner.

"I'm really grateful Milo has friends like you. I didn't." Renner pulled the keys out of the ignition and climbed out of the car. "Or maybe I didn't try to find them. But either way, I'm…grateful that you would accost me in a parking lot on his behalf. He deserves it."

"Do you deserve him?" Vaughn asked.

That was the million-dollar question, wasn't it? Renner's knee-jerk answer was no. Not before he'd fucked up. And not after. But the answer wasn't so simple. If he wanted a chance with Milo, he *had* to deserve him. Had to *make* himself worthy. Because the man he loved would get nothing less than 1,000 percent.

"I'm going to make sure I can answer yes to that next time you ask me." Renner had a hard time saying what came next, but he would have done anything to guarantee he fixed the damage he'd done to his relationship with Milo. "And…I may need some help. From you both."

"I bet that was tough for you to say," Duke rumbled through a smile, laying a hand on his shoulder. "If it makes things easier, we'll agree to help for Milo's sake."

"Yes." Renner started to brush off Duke's hand, but gave his brother-in-law an appreciative nod instead. "That would be ideal."

...

Renner was gone. *Still* gone.

After Boston, he'd just...left. Probably hadn't even detoured through Jersey on his way back to Manhattan, or Milo would have heard about it by now.

People in Hook—mainly his coworkers—were perceptive, and the looks of sympathy he'd been getting throughout the week had been...comforting, actually. He wanted the hurt to be visible, because it made him feel less alone. Made facing the day less daunting. Furthermore, their disappointment as word spread that Renner had jetted off to his next enterprise meant they not only accepted Milo, but they'd been cheering him and Renner on from the sidelines. For how long?

Had their attraction to each other been obvious before either one of them realized it? Maybe if Milo had recognized the part of himself that responded to Renner sooner, he wouldn't have fucked up by bringing Travis into the picture. Maybe Renner never would have questioned his dedication and they would be together right now. Milo wouldn't feel like there was a mile-wide gash across his middle, worrying about Renner. Missing him like a motherfucker. Positive with each passing minute that he'd made a mistake.

God, the regret was fierce. Walking away from Renner in Boston had seemed like the only option, even though the cards were finally laid out on the table. Now Milo wasn't sure.

It would have been so easy to accept Renner's apology. To trust he wouldn't freak out on him again or put him through another test. Milo had known from the beginning that Renner needed someone who refused to be deterred. Someone who would keep coming back *no matter what.* When it really counted, Milo had turned and walked, instead of assuring Renner he would never burn him like that asshole from his past. Making him *believe* and *trust* that they were solid. Unmovable.

Unable to take another second staring at the dark office above the factory floor, Milo went into the break room, getting a soda from the vending machine. He rolled it across his forehead. This constant feeling that he was drifting, without a place to touch down, was getting worse. Five days without Renner's sarcasm. Without those hawk eyes on him as he passed through the machinery, doing his rounds. Without that feeling of security that Renner had robbed him of in the end. He needed it back. Needed to give it to Renner in return.

Vaughn would let him go home early if Milo asked. He should just go home and...sleep? Not likely. He'd logged more hours staring at his bedroom ceiling in the last five days than were healthy. The only thing that helped so far was whiskey, which had backfired by reminding him of Renner, leaving him a god-awful combination of drunk and wired.

Fuck this. He was going to Manhattan tonight.

Just making the decision was like a breath of fresh air. Even if he only fought with Renner and solved nothing, it would be better than waiting and wondering if they were over.

Don't let this be over. How can it be over when I'm this ill over being without him?

The break room door opened and a woman walked in, safety goggles perched on top of her head. "What are you doing still in here?" She winked at him. "Haven't you heard the boss is back?"

"What?" Milo lunged to his feet, sending his chair crashing into the stainless steel refrigerator. "When?"

"Just strolled in."

"How would I have heard?"

The woman shrugged. "The walls in this place have ears, don't they?"

She launched into a rundown of the latest gossip, but Milo heard none of it. Renner was just going to *stroll* in after five days of silence? Without any kind of warning? Jesus, maybe heart problems were contagious, because his was racing at an alarming rate. All of a sudden, he wasn't sad about the last five days, he was pissed about them. Pointless. They'd both been idiots and Renner was about to *hear* it. Milo didn't care if the whole damn *factory* heard.

Head of steam in full effect, Milo threw open the break room door and charged toward the staircase that would lead to Renner's office...

But Milo stopped on a dime—bombs going off in his ears—when his gaze landed on the man himself. Renner stood in his usual spot in the upstairs office, hands clasped behind his back, watching Milo approach from behind the glass. *Holy shit*, Milo got so dizzy with relief, he almost hit the deck. There he was. Here. *Close.*

That was before Milo got closer and saw Renner's appearance.

He looked...*ravaged*. Was he sick? At the very least, the man was exhausted and...yeah, miserable. Milo could see that, and it was like an ice pick entering his heart.

Milo started jogging, needing to get up the stairs, but the sound of Renner's voice in surround sound forced him to slow again. He looked up to see Renner had lifted the intercom receiver to his mouth, addressing the entire factory at once. It was only then Milo realized the machinery was humming, but not active. A quick glance told him every worker was front and center, as if they'd been expecting Renner to speak. What was happening?

"I have an announcement." Milo's insides damn near melted at the sound of Renner's husky tone, even though it was further proof of his exhaustion. He was usually so brisk. "This might come as a shock to all of you, but it came to my attention recently that I don't know everything." Laughter spread across the floor. "There was a new client I was attempting to win over…and manufacturing that client's products would have meant more jobs. Here in Hook. It would have meant even better facilities. Things that are important to you…have become important to me, too."

How long could Milo stand there listening to Renner be so honest without exploding? Apparently they would find out, because his feet were glued to the floor, his pulse going crazy.

"Things that seem right sometimes…aren't, however," Renner continued. "Namely, this client. And I never would have found that out on my own. Never. Not without someone giving me a good kick in the ass." Briefly, Renner's attention landed on Milo before cutting away. "Thanks to this person, I found another way to give this town what it deserves."

Renner had to wait for the cheering to die down after that. It was so loud, Milo worried it might break windows, but the workers quieted again when Renner held up a hand.

"I've purchased another site five miles from here. As soon as the working environment has been deemed safe, I'll be hiring directly out of Hook." Louder cheering, high-fiving, and in some cases, even tears. Milo could admit to being close to them himself. Renner's gaze landed hard on him…and everyone seemed to fall silent, although the buzz of energy was incredible. Unable to be suppressed. Nothing, though, compared to the thunderclaps going off in Milo's chest. One after the other. "I could lie and claim I'll be staying in Hook to oversee the project, but I'm staying for you, Milo. I'll stay forever…for you. If you think I work too hard now? Get ready, because I won't rest until I have you back. Until you know for goddamn sure I'll never let you go again."

Love and a sense of completion pushed in on Milo from all sides. He had no choice but to start laughing or embarrass himself, but the laughter was happy. So happy. He actually had to slap a hand over his eyes because the vision of Renner laying himself bare was too much. So much he worried the organ in his chest might give out from working so much overtime.

And that was before the music started.

From the rear of the gathered workers, a burst of loud Latin-flavored music began, turning everyone's heads, including Milo's. When he saw Duke holding an outdated boom box and Vaughn giving a thumbs-up, Milo only laughed harder, although he had no idea what was going on. Until a familiar scent found his nose…and he turned to find Renner standing beside him, obviously having left the office and descended the stairs.

Up close, he appeared even more haggard, but his eyes were alive. Alive as Milo felt.

"Dance with me?"

Milo drew in a slow, shaky breath, ready to throw himself into Renner's arms, but needing a second to compose himself. "You don't dance."

"I do now. I do everything for you." The crowd closed in around them, not even bothering to be subtle about eavesdropping. "I'll do anything. Just let me keep you."

"I guess I have to," Milo responded, heart in his throat. "Considering I love you and someone needs to make sure you take care of yourself."

Renner didn't appear to be breathing as he stepped closer, leaving them only an inch apart. "Say that first part again."

Milo moved in and pressed their foreheads together. "I

love you, Renner."

A low, vibrating curse. "I wasn't even sure you would take me back, now you give me this?" He took Milo's hand and brought it to his chest, right over his pounding heart. "When am I going to stop underestimating you?"

"I did the underestimating this time," Milo said. "What you said…"

"I meant every word." One of Renner's hands slipped through his hair, the other drawing him close. "I'm staying here for you. This is going to be home, because it's where you are. If I go somewhere, I'm taking you with me. No days or nights apart. Not because I don't have trust. But because I don't have the patience for time without Milo. I don't want to know what that's like anymore. I *need* you."

To someone else, Renner's heavy hand might have been too much. Too selfish. But it was finally—*finally*—exactly what Milo needed to hear. To feel.

"Never apart," Milo agreed, happiness sprinting through his blood. "Never again."

They both smiled, their mouths lifting right up against each other. Then Renner surprised Milo again by taking him by the hand…and spinning him around.

They danced.

And everyone joined them.

Epilogue

Six months later

Damn, Milo was one lovesick puppy.

Honestly. There was no other way to describe a man who'd dug his boyfriend's dress shirt out of the laundry basket, buried his face in the familiar smell, and started jerking off to beat the fucking band. Renner had only been gone on the business trip for three days, but since Milo usually went along, the separation had been *hard*. A lot like his dick, which was in such dire need of Renner, Milo swore he'd heard it crying softly in the middle of the night.

He would be with Renner in Hong Kong right now if the new factory branch hadn't required one of them to remain in Hook to oversee some key machinery installations. And while Milo was proud as hell of the new plant, he couldn't help but resent anything that kept him away from his man. Three nights spent alone in their new house—just down the street from Duke and Samantha—was more than enough. He wanted Renner home *yesterday*.

Milo fell onto the bed facedown, lifting his ass and visualizing Renner kneeling behind him. His boyfriend's gruff commands played in his mind while his fist violated his erection, stroking at warp speed. *Pants off. Show me where the hurt is. Open yourself up for me. Tell me, baby, who's the only one allowed to ride this pretty-boy ass?* He opened his mouth against the shirt collar, letting his tongue flick out, trying to catch Renner's taste as well as smell.

The whir of the ceiling fan sent cool air down onto his sweating bare back. Onto his straining thighs. His pained face. "Fuck me. Please. You're the only one."

"Damn right I am," came Renner's rasping voice from the bedroom doorway. "Have to say, this is one hell of a welcome home."

It was ridiculous to feel like a kid caught with his hand in the cookie jar, especially after six months of living together. Despite the all-encompassing relief and excitement at his boyfriend's arrival, however, heat crept over Milo's face, a combination of anticipation and, yeah, blushing. "You weren't supposed to be home for another two days."

"You're making sweet love to my shirt, baby." Humor, love, hunger threaded through his tone. "I doubt you're complaining."

Milo flopped over onto his back and used the shirt to hide his swollen dick, using every measure of his willpower to stop beating himself off. Not because he was all that embarrassed, but because he wanted Renner to come closer. *Immediately.* And hiding any part of himself tended to make that happen pretty damn fast.

On cue, Renner's right eyebrow arched. Suitcase forgotten at his feet, precise fingers lifted to unknot his tie. "I just crammed in thirteen meetings back to back and paid through the nose to switch my flight, because I can barely make it through the day without you." The tie dropped and he began to work the buttons of his shirt, while Milo's heart pumped wildly in his throat. "When I know you won't be with me at the end of the day, I forget people's names and where I'm supposed to be. I stare off into space. My feet won't move. I'm a mess. A useless, good-for-nothing mess." The shirt dropped, revealing those incredible shoulders. "I just walked in to find you licking my shirt and talking to me, thinking I'm thousands of miles away. You need me as badly as I need you. You have any clue what that does to me?"

"I can guess," Milo responded, hoarse from listening to the speech. At some point during Renner's words, he'd sat up, the shirt falling away from his lap, forgotten. "I'm fucking glad you're back, boss man. I'm just bones and blood when you're not around."

The light of affection flickered in Renner's eyes before his voice cracked like a belt, swift and rife with feeling. Milo felt it across his stomach, down his spine. "Get over here and tell me properly."

A rush of starvation made Milo light-headed, his johnson glancing off his thigh as he knelt, walking to the edge of the bed on his knees. Before he reached the end of the mattress, however, Renner surged forward and knocked Milo onto his back, landing on top of him. The groans they loosed into each other's mouths were those of two wounded beasts trying to find the source of their pain. Just as they both needed, Renner aggressed, grappling with Milo's wrists and holding them down hard above his head, while Milo helplessly rolled his hips, humping his boyfriend and begging for relief with nonsensical words.

"I'll never forget seeing your face buried in my shirt," Renner grated, reaching down to unfasten his own pants with a wince. "Worth every sleepless night to make it back early, just for that. Hated seeing you miserable, missing me, but goddamn me, I loved it, too."

"Slept in one of them, too. It's on the bathroom floor." Milo finished the admission on a gasp when Renner bent forward, sinking his teeth into Milo's pectoral muscle. "Wore your cologne, listened to your old Robert Johnson albums. Another day and I would've resorted to eating your shitty health cereal. I love you, all right? Don't be surprised by me fucking your shirt."

"Don't be surprised by me busting my ass to come home early," Renner returned, his eyes and voice so full of emotion, Renner couldn't get an honest breath. "I love you, too."

With their mouths and foreheads pressed together, Renner scooped up the bottle of lube still lying on the bed, using it liberally on their lower bodies, sliding his blunt, perfect fingers into every dip and swell. Using it to pump his fist up and down Milo's cock, until Milo was pushing with desperate grunts into his hand. Renner's lips locked together with Milo's, falling into a rough pattern of kissing that grew more aggressive with every tongue stroke, every gruff moan of pleasure.

Milo had woken up horny as hell, hence the solo session, but by the time Renner took their hard cocks in one hand, jerking them off in the same powerful fist, his goddamn balls were full of such punishing pressure, he didn't know if he'd make it any longer. *"Please, please, please,"* Milo near-shouted, head thrown back, neck muscles straining. "Need you. I'm dying."

"No, I won't let you." Renner breathed heavily. "I was dead when you found me, and you'll *never* feel that way. Not as long as I'm full of this life you gave me." Milo reeled, his chest aching with pure love, but Renner didn't give him time to revel. Later, he would, but not now. "Lift up, baby. Ankles crossed behind my back. Going to give you three days worth of fucking." He growled against the seam of Milo's lips. "You're going to take it this way, then I'm going to bury your face in my shirt again and do it harder."

Milo's cock released a hot bead of come, every muscle in his stomach constricting to the point of agony, but he managed to follow his boyfriend's strict instructions, raising his legs and locking them together. "You going to say thank you afterward?" Milo murmured gruffly.

Renner's mouth ticked up. "If you don't remind me to take my heart pills, I'll think about it."

Any doubts about Renner's constantly improving health were obliterated a moment later when he pumped his cock into Milo's ass, momentarily knocking every coherent thought from his mind. *Jesus*, if six months had passed and Milo still hadn't gotten used to his man's throbbing size pressing in and stretching, hitting that pressure point that made his eyes tear, made his balls draw up and shudder, he never would. *Fine*. He didn't give a fuck. It was new and mind-blowing every time, Renner's big chest heaving on top of him, the pendulum of his balls smacking against his ass like a spanking. Enforcing. Owning him.

"I love my life," Milo gasped. "Holy shit, it's amazing."

Renner's drives lost their rhythm a second, that once-rare, full-bodied laugh filling their bedroom. It cut off when he ground deep on a groan and met Milo's gaze. "If I ever give you a reason to call it anything less than amazing, you tell me."

"Come on now." Milo gripped the strands of Renner's hair, hauling him down for a kiss. "You damn well know I will."

Both men smiled, because they knew that day would never come to pass. Neither of them would let it. And then Renner's bucking thrusts kicked up again, his eyes clenching shut, teeth bared as he slaked his lust. It took only five strokes of Milo's own dick to send come shooting free, coating his chest and belly, the relief out of this world, depleting him.

Renner watched the spurting mess make itself and as Milo knew it would, the sight got him off with a strangled moan, before he fell onto Milo, muttering *thank-yous* into his neck.

"Welcome home, boss man." Milo yawned, smacking Renner on the ass and getting a poke in the ribs in response. "Now, about round two with the shirt—"

The phone rang.

Renner had been in the process of beginning a wet French kiss of Milo's eager mouth, but pulled back now with a heartfelt, *"Fuck."*

Renner sat back and reached into the pocket of his pants, retrieving his cell. "It's Sam." He punched the screen, answering his sister's call. "Make it good, sis."

Milo shot into a sitting position when Samantha's scream echoed around the room. *"Renner!"*

The color drained from the factory owner's face. "What?"

"How does a baby get food when it's hungry?"

"What? How?"

"Womb service."

A long pause wherein Milo and Renner exchanged a terrified look. "Oh God," Renner said, both of them already lunging off the bed. "The baby is coming?"

"I knew you'd get it." Samantha sighed. Then she broke off into another scream.

"We're on the way," Renner and Milo shouted.

• • •

Renner's brother-in-law, Duke, was the first person they saw upon arrival.

It wasn't a pretty scene.

"Stop telling me to watch SportsCenter," Duke bellowed, sending nurses running in every direction. In one giant hand, he held a baby car seat, in the other, a stuffed teddy bear.

Prepared for everything, as usual. Except his beloved wife going through labor, apparently.

"It was your wife's idea, Mr. Crawford," the doctor explained patiently. "She thought it might calm you down."

"I don't *want* to be calm. I want my Samantha to stop crying."

The doctor tilted his head. "She's having a *baby*, sir."

"Oh, you don't say?" Duke did a double take when he saw Milo and Renner jogging in his direction. "This guy says Samantha is having a *baby*. He must have some kind of fancy medical degree." He turned back to the doctor. "The kind that should have taught him how to take one tiny woman's pain away."

The doctor disappeared back into the room.

A fresh scream tore through the corridor—one Renner recognized as his sister's. If Renner hadn't been standing right in front of his brother-in-law, he never would have believed it when Duke started to cry. Not all-out sobbing or anything so unmanly. It was one of those repeated swallowing and clearing of the throat kind of cries. But his eyes were damp, his giant chest looking like it could blow any second.

"What do I do?" Duke asked, splitting a look between Renner and Milo. "I don't know what to do. I'm supposed to be in there, but I think I'm only making it worse for Sam."

Honest to God, before Milo, Renner would have thrown money at someone in the hospital to remedy the whole situation. Which *might* have included Duke in a straitjacket. But there was no sweeping aside the importance of *people* anymore. Their kaleidoscope of feelings and faults and...the ties they'd created inside him. The love Milo had brought into his life made him aware of the love all around him. His sister. Yes, even Duke. Maybe *especially* Duke at that very moment, just because he needed the extra support more than anybody.

It was no surprise to Renner that Milo threw an arm

around Duke and shook him. "Come on, man. It's game time. The *championship*. Hours of *SportsCenter* have brought you to this moment." He pointed at the hospital room door. "Go in there and be coach of the year."

"Okay, sure," Renner said. "Sports references. I can get in on this." He pried the car seat and stuffed toy out of Duke's white-knuckled grip, setting them down. "There's only one minute left on the scoreboard. Go in there and knock the pins down."

Duke sighed. "That was terrible."

Renner winked to let the big man know he'd been joking. "Hey, you're the badass who ran into an exploding factory. This should be a piece of cake."

"Yeah. Well, you're the one who ran in after me," Duke returned, his face full of dawning warmth. "So if I die from sympathy pains before the day is over, you're fully capable of helping Sam change diapers in my place."

"Don't get carried away," Renner said, his chest expanding at the sound of Milo's laugh. "Go in there and bring out your daughter." He sent his boyfriend a disbelieving smile. "Our niece."

"Holy shit, a girl," Duke breathed. "Another female in the house."

With that, the giant mechanic ducked into the delivery room. Through the door, the unmistakable sounds of *SportsCenter* could be heard, followed by Duke's adamant, "*Turn it off.*"

Renner and Milo were still laughing minutes later when River and Vaughn came speed-walking down the hallway, their little daughter Marcy in tow, Vaughn holding a fistful of pink cigars. They all moved quietly to the family room and waited. Renner's heart damn near exploded when Milo sat down with Marcy and helped her complete a scene in her Disney princess coloring book, making her giggle with character impressions. Seriously, his Olaf was spot on. Was there anything his man couldn't do?

If they hadn't been interrupted earlier, Renner had planned to spend the evening a *very* different way. He hadn't been embellishing when he told Milo he'd been a mess the last few days. Something had been missing when he left. A promise. Certain words. But he hadn't put a name to the feeling until a client had caught Renner's attention by twisting his wedding ring during the meeting. A platinum band was burning a hole in the inside of Renner's jacket pocket right now, and when the time was right, he'd beg Milo to be his husband.

The waiting room door burst open and Duke staggered in. "She's beautiful. Oh my God, she's beautiful. Both of them are. *Jesus.*"

A cheer went up around the room, cigars were passed out, hugs were exchanged, and tears were shed. And later on that night, when everything had settled down and Sam was resting peacefully with baby Laine, Renner found a dark corner of the hospital and asked Milo to be his world. Officially and always. The question was barely out of his mouth before Milo said yes.

And the friends all lived ridiculously happy lives, forever after.

Until their daughters got old enough to date.

Acknowledgments

Thank you *so* much to all the readers who picked up the Made in Jersey series. It feels as though I just started writing it— and bam, it's already over. When I started writing the series, Renner Bastion's story was a gray, hazy blotch. I always have a strong sense of every series character's storyline, but his didn't come to me right away. I made notes, discarded them. Tried different plot lines. I'd never written two men together before, and I suppose that's why the story took longer to compose itself. But it was a beautiful thing when Milo hit the scene and the story came into focus. I wanted to skip ahead and write Renner's book so many times, because I couldn't wait to reform the supposed villain with the help of Milo's fresh, guileless spirit. It's really difficult to leave this Hook family behind, but I do so knowing they'll triumph, fail, and persevere together, living their HEAs to the fullest.

Thank you to my editor Heather Howland! This is our twentieth damn book together. It's crazy to think about where we started, editing Derek Tyler and sharing the reactions when *actual people* with *real eyeballs* were reading the book. I still get those goose bumps when a book releases, but nothing will compare to that first voyage. I owe Heather for pulling me out of the slush pile and giving me a chance, which is why I've dedicated this book to her.

Thank you, as always, to my husband, Patrick, and daughter, Mackenzie. I've only recently come through a four-and-a-half-year writing binge, with hardly any breaks, and they stood by me and cheered me on the whole time. When I started writing seriously, I did it so my daughter might be proud of me someday, when she's old enough to understand the work that goes into writing a book. That's still my hope, with every word I type.

Thank you to author Christina Lee, who read an early version of *Wound Tight* and gave me some great feedback. I really appreciate it! You're such a kind, encouraging person and a talented writer.

Thank you to photographer Lindee Robinson for the awesome cover shot!

And finally…as always, thank you to Bailey's Babes for supporting me and keeping me encouraged every day of the week!

About the Author

New York Times and USA TODAY bestselling author Tessa Bailey lives in Brooklyn, New York, with her husband and young daughter. When she isn't writing or reading romance, she enjoys a good argument and thirty-minute recipes.

www.tessabailey.com
Join Bailey's Babes!

RAW REDEMPTION

BOILING POINT

OWNED BY FATE

EXPOSED BY FATE

DRIVEN BY FATE

HARD COMPROMISE
a *Compromise Me* novel by Samanthe Beck

Laurie Peterson assumes her impulsive one-night stand with sinfully sexy Sheriff Ethan Booker is the biggest surprise of the year...until her bakery burns down while she's basking in the afterglow. It looks like her dreams are up in smoke, but then Ethan proposes a deal too tempting to resist.

HIS BEST MISTAKE
a *Shillings Agency* novel by Diane Alberts

One night with a stranger... Security expert Mark Matthews has loved, and lost, and has no intention of ever loving again — especially not a woman who thrives on her life being in danger. Now, hot, meaningless sex with strangers he had no intention of ever seeing again? That's a whole other story. And it's all life as a single father allows him to enjoy. But when he meets Daisy O'Rourke, the game is on, because she's everything he swore to stay away from. She has bad idea written all over her, but he's in too deep to walk away now...

A Fool for You
a *Foolproof Love* novel by Katee Robert

It's been thirteen years since Hope Moore left Devil's Falls, land of sexy cowboys and bad memories. Back for the weekend, she has no intention of seeing Daniel Rodriguez, the man she never got over, or for the two of them getting down and dirty. It's just a belated goodbye, right? No harm, no foul. Until six weeks later, when her pregnancy test comes back positive…

Playing it Cool
a *Sydney Smoke Rugby* novel by Amy Andrews

Harper Nugent might have a little extra junk in her trunk, but her stepbrother calling her out on it is the last straw… When rugby hottie, Dexter Blake, witnesses the insult, he surprises Harper by asking her out. In front of her dumbass brother. Score! Of course, she knows it's not for reals, but Dex won't take no for an answer. Still the date is better than either expected. So is the next one. And the next. And the heat between them…sizzles their clothes right off. Suddenly, this fake relationship is feeling all too real…

Printed in Great Britain
by Amazon

24686518R00118